"Why are you sitting in the dark?" She reached for the light switch.

"Don't," he said, his voice throaty. "Leave the light off."

"Why?"

He rose from the chair and moved toward her. Was he still upset with her? "What are you doing?"

He came closer, silent. A shaft of moonlight flashed across his war-torn face. When he was less than a foot from her, he stopped. Even in the darkness, his presence overwhelmed her, made her light headed. The scent of his cologne mingled with leather.

"In the darkness, you can't see my scar. In the darkness, we're the same."

Camille's eyes welled. Trembling, she slid her hand to her throat. "Romeo," she whispered, "I never meant to hurt you."

ELIZABETH GODDARD is a seventh-generation Texan who recently spent five years in beautiful Southern Oregon, which serves as a setting for some of her novels. She is now back in East Texas, living near her family. When she's not writing, she's busy homeschooling her four children. Beth is the author of several novels and novellas. She's actively involved in several writing organizations including American Christian Fiction Writers (ACFW) and loves to mentor new writers.

Books by Elizabeth Goddard

HEARTSONG PRESENTS
HP777—Seasons of Love
HP893—Disarming Andi
HP913—Exposing Amber
HP933—Praying for Rayne

Under the Redwood Tree

Elizabeth Goddard

Heartsong Presents

To the military men and women who serve this great country.
To the loved ones who wait and pray at home.
May He hold you in His hands.
To my amazing husband and children—
I could not do this without your encouragement and support.
To Shannon McNear who tirelessly reads my
stories without fail—thank you, dear friend.

A note from the Author:
*I love to hear from my readers! You may correspond with
me by writing:*

Elizabeth Goddard
Author Relations
PO Box 721
Uhrichsville, OH 44683

ISBN 978-1-61626-538-0

UNDER THE REDWOOD TREE

Scripture taken from the New American Standard Bible, © 1960, 1962, 1963, 1968, 1971, 1972, 1973, 1975, 1977, 1995 by The Lockman Foundation. Used by permission.

This book is a work of fiction. Names, characters, places, and incidents are either products of the author's imagination or used fictitiously.

Our mission is to publish and distribute inspirational products offering exceptional value and biblical encouragement to the masses.

PRINTED IN THE U.S.A.

one

She'd always called him her handsome Romeo.

Not anymore.

Wind rushed by as he squeezed the throttle, accelerating the blue and silver Suzuki Hayabusa—the world's fastest motorcycle. The bike rocketed forward, racing to the top of the hill on the California back road, and just as he hoped, he became airborne after cresting the rise.

Asphalt rose fast to greet him as the machine he straddled joined with the road. The snakelike highway that wound through redwood state park near the Oregon border was almost behind him, and with it, his last push for speed before slowing.

Too soon he would approach the small Northern California town of Redbrook, where his mother now lived with a friend.

Romeo Merete had avoided Mama far too long already. For at least a year he'd toured the country on his own, putting off the day when he would see her face-to-face. Dodging the day when she would see what he'd become. Though he missed her and knew his avoidance had hurt her, he also believed he was sparing her by hiding the truth.

In that way he was being a good son, though she wouldn't understand.

It was time to confront the inevitable. Besides, Romeo had a job offer in Arizona and was running out of time. It was now or never.

His palms grew moist inside his gloves as he squeezed the handlebar and slowed the motorcycle to a manageable speed. Small-town neighborhood speeds.

Was he finally ready?

No muse stirred Camille Westover with inspiration to paint. The large white square stared at her from across the room.

The thirty-by-thirty empty canvas cried out for golden hues of raw umber and burnt sienna, for cerulean blue and crimson alizarin, for creamy textures and strong pigmentations applied with emotion and artistic skill.

But Camille had already spent her energies on another painting—one of her favorite places in the world—a particular giant redwood tree. She loved sitting under that tree, so why couldn't she get it right?

She meandered over to the easel where the oil painting rested tall, mocking her. She examined it with her artist's eye, angling her head this way and that.

Under the Redwood Tree. The title for her painting was drawn from a song Shakespeare had written for his play *As You Like It.* The song was called "Under the Greenwood Tree" and was about living in the country and enjoying nature, throwing ambition to the wind.

"What's the problem?" Aunt Erin stood next to her, angling her head as well.

"I didn't hear you come in," Camille said. Pragmatic as her aunt was, Camille adored the woman. She'd come to live with Aunt Erin at sixteen, only five years ago, when her mother died. Camille's sisters were already on their own. Sela was married, and Alexa attended Columbia University on a scholarship.

"It's missing something, don't you think?" Camille asked.

"What could it be missing? It looks every bit like the photograph there." Aunt Erin indicated the photo Camille had taken of the redwood tree. A place Camille often went to think and pray.

"Emotion. Spirit. Romance. . ." Camille turned her back on the painting. "It's completely dead and uninspiring."

Aunt Erin shook her head and waved her hand, dismissing

Camille's opinion. "You and your artsy ways. Romance doesn't have anything to do with it. You need to find some new inspiration, that's all. But how are you going to paint something else in time to enter the contest?"

Camille drew in a long breath. "I don't know, but I have every intention of winning." Considering that Camille had won every art competition she'd entered, this opportunity seemed like her chance to finally make her way. Even Aunt Erin thought it was a sure thing.

The Redwood Art Association had invited judges from around the world to judge the art contest. The winner would be awarded a scholarship to the Art Institute of Chicago—a prestigious school ranked one of the top fine-art schools in the country. Nothing less would do if she was to hold her own against her sister Alexa.

To date, Camille had attended a local community college but had failed to gain the necessary finances or scholarships required to attend anything as esteemed as Columbia University. Alexa had attended Columbia on a full scholarship.

She exhaled, knowing that the painting wasn't good enough to win, and not winning meant not getting the scholarship. She hated to think of the look on Alexa's face if that happened. Or didn't happen. She hated being second best when they were growing up, and she hated her need to compete now.

"You're meant for bigger things. . . ."

Camille believed Alexa, but at twenty-one, she feared this was her one chance to make it happen, and that scared her. Right now, she lived with Aunt Erin to share expenses, teaching art classes and making purses. Plenty of people she knew had to work more than one job. She wasn't any different.

"In the meantime, those purses are not going to move themselves off the shelves." Aunt Erin snapped Camille's thoughts back to reality. "Camille, be practical. You have a business to run here. Get out and sell those purses. Better yet, try eBay."

A glance around the room brought on a deluge of stress—Aunt Erin was right. Camille had her hand-crafted bags to finish. She'd already put a lot of money into a website to sell them.

"What if I add a line of dresses? Maybe I could add them to the website and call them *Romantically Yours*."

Aunt Erin, who had never liked Camille's eye for fashion, snorted. "You mean like those dresses you prefer? Hippie wear? You have your hands dipped in too many things. You're a collage—an unfocused hodgepodge of random things."

"Oh, is that what I am?" Camille sighed, wishing Aunt Erin appreciated her artistic side. "I need to get to work now."

"But it's seven o'clock. Stella's preparing peppermint tea and biscotti. That's why I came up to the attic. To ask if you'd join us."

Peppermint tea? Camille couldn't stomach the stuff. She placed a hand over her midsection and shook her head. "After that huge plate of spaghetti, I couldn't eat another bite."

Aunt Erin headed for the door. Just before she disappeared, she glanced back at Camille, her eyes flashing disapproval. Then affection softened her expression. "You need to get out of the attic more."

"Thanks. I'll keep that in mind." Camille grinned.

The large room situated above her aunt's Victorian home was the perfect place for Camille's paintings. Her aunt had called the space Camille's Attic, and the name officially caught. The designer handbags she created sold under a label with the same name. Perfect, except. . . She wanted something more. She needed to be out on her own, not prodded like she was a child. She needed to be successful like Alexa, but deep inside, she feared proving herself wouldn't be good enough this time, either.

❧

In the waning light of day, Romeo guided his motorcycle

through the quiet neighborhood, grateful he hadn't chosen a modified Harley. Even the low rumble pouring from his Hayabusa made him feel conspicuous at a time when he needed stealth. Victorian homes lined the streets in shades of gray and pale blues, accented in pinks, greens, and earth tones. He could never have found the house where his mother now lived if he were simply looking for the Victorian house on Fern Street. Good thing he'd written down the complete address.

He pulled into the driveway and turned off the engine. Both feet on the ground, he remained seated. They said that time healed all wounds, and true enough, he'd grown calloused at the sight of his face in the mirror. It no longer disturbed him. If only others' reactions would stop bothering him. Watching his mother's expression once she saw him would be like reliving the ordeal all over again.

If he hadn't been thousands of miles and an ocean away, she probably could have remained in Indiana and kept the family restaurant going. Romeo would have had something to come home to. And then, he could get on with his life. Instead, she'd sold the place and moved across the country to live with a longtime friend.

A pang struck his heart. Did he really think he could just pick up where things left off? He wanted his old life back— for things to be normal.

He hopped off his bike and strode toward the door, ignoring the pounding in his chest. He refused to feel sorry for himself.

As he lifted his fist to knock, fear wound through his core. Was he doing the right thing? What if she wasn't home? What if he'd come at a bad time? He steeled himself.

Doing the right thing was hardly ever easy.

two

On the porch of the old Victorian home, Romeo waited and prepared himself for Mama's reaction. Usually there was a quick widening of the eyes and a furtive look away. Or a stony expression, an attempt to ignore the obvious.

A wreath of orange and blue flowers hung on the door, partially covering the glass, as if to say the home was warm and inviting. When no one answered, Romeo knocked a second time and pressed the doorbell. From outside, he couldn't hear the telltale ring. Was it even working?

He'd picked the wrong day and time to show up on his mother's doorstep. Correction. His mother's friend's doorstep. He hadn't told her he was coming. Served him right, if nobody was home.

Romeo sagged a little. He peeked through the glass at the neat and cozy foyer. But that was a little intrusive. When he backed away, his reflection in the window stared back at him. He jammed his hands in his pockets and turned away from the door *and* the reflection, which seemed to mock him.

Might as well explore. The ladies could be sitting in the backyard for all he knew. He stepped off the porch and perused a front yard overflowing with pink pansies, purple petunias, purple and white hydrangeas, and all manner of floral artistry accented with garden gnomes. His mother definitely had a hand in this garden, except that it looked like something from folklore or a fairy tale. A few topiary trees in animal form stood as sentries.

Mama and her friend might not be aware of his arrival, but a quick glance at the houses next door and across the street told him the neighbors were watching. He'd seen movement behind one or two curtains.

The house was entirely too quiet. Romeo didn't want to be seen as a trespasser. He definitely should have called ahead. His cell phone was dead at the moment, so there wasn't any way he could call now.

As Romeo began the trek around the side of the house, he glanced through the windows to see if anyone was inside. Regret squirmed in his stomach. If only he could see his mother alone for the first time and not have to witness her reaction in the company of others.

He swiped a hand down his face. Maybe this wasn't such a great idea, after all.

Surely he'd made enough noise when he rode up on his motorcycle. If anyone were home, they would have heard him.

❧

Sitting at her desk in the attic, Camille listened to music and sipped coffee while she proofread the latest post for her blog, *In Love with Shakespeare*. Though she'd told Aunt Erin she needed to work, her aunt would disapprove and just pigeonhole the blog as frivolous romantic fluff.

Camille smiled as she read her blog post from last night. Every evening she read a scene from Shakespeare and then posted her thoughts on her blog. ·

I had rather hear my dog bark at a crow than a man swear he loves me.

Shakespeare's character Beatrice shared Aunt Erin's sentiment. Camille's aunt claimed she didn't want or need a man's love. So, she'd never married.

But Camille wondered what it would be like to love and be loved.

Though she considered the words between Beatrice and Benedick on the witty side of biting, the two were definitely playing on the edge of amorous feelings in *Much Ado about Nothing*.

Scratching could not make it worse, an 'twere such a face as yours were.

And Beatrice's comment regarding Benedick only made Camille believe he must be a handsome soldier. If only she could meet one, she certainly wouldn't scare him off with a sharp tongue like Beatrice's.

Camille leaned back and pushed the PUBLISH POST button. "And I'll bet they fall in love in the end."

After only a few weeks, she was surprised to see how many followers she'd garnered. It was sort of like a book club about Shakespeare, with the blog open for comments and discussion. There were three comments to her post already.

Several discussed Shakespeare's double meanings. Delighted, she skimmed through the rest. The last one seemed off topic and snagged her.

There is no measure in the occasion that breeds; therefore the sadness is without limit. Signed, Don John.

Someone had chosen a screen name from the villain in *Much Ado about Nothing.*

An unusual post, to be sure.

Camille sighed, uncertain if the comment warranted a reply. She shoved her chair back from the desk. Her gaze drifted to the empty canvas, a stiff reminder that she was on the verge of failure.

She closed her eyes and prayed for new inspiration.

When she opened them, she glanced out the window, the shadows stretching in the evening light. A stranger dressed in black leather stalked around the side of the house. Losing sight of him, Camille rushed to another window, this one gabled. In the backyard, he stood in the shadows.

For all of five seconds, Camille was paralyzed as her mind tried to comprehend what was happening.

Alarm set her in motion. She whipped through the attic door and down the steps, calling out for the other two women.

"Aunt Erin! Stella. . ." At the bottom of the steps, she called through the house, "There's someone in the backyard. Where are you?"

She ran to the living room where they had been watching a sitcom, but the television wasn't on, and the two weren't there. At the back of the house, Camille slowly opened the french doors to the deck, where they often drank their tea. But no one was there.

No one except. . .

The stranger froze when he saw her.

Camille's gaze traveled over the left side of his face—scarred and deformed. She looked down, ashamed that she'd stared.

Then she remembered—he was intruding. "Who are you?" Her voice trembled. "I've already called the police."

She bit her lip, wishing she'd done just that. Maybe the warning would be enough.

The man's grave expression startled, looking surprised before a deep sadness crept into his eyes. His pain was palpable, and she wished she could take back her harsh words. Why had she been so quick to judge him? Still, she took a wobbly step back, uncertain about his intentions.

From somewhere behind Camille, Stella spoke, her voice a mere whisper. "Romeo, is that you?"

ঽ

Romeo was a statue, unable to move. Unable to speak.

On the inside, he almost crumpled. *Lord, to face her for the first time, I needed to be alone with her. . . .*

If only the beautiful young woman hadn't seen him first. He'd hoped and prayed to become accustomed to people's reactions. Oh, he was accustomed all right, but her strained expression still cut through him.

"Romeo," his mother said, taking a step forward. "My son."

Romeo wanted to make a move toward her, but his legs

wouldn't budge. His feet had become hardened on the deck. "Hello, Mama."

As she closed the distance between them, he noticed how slowly she moved. Was she displeased at seeing him? Was he an embarrassment?

Finally, standing almost toe-to-toe with him, she lifted her hands and cupped his face. Turning the left side of his face toward her, she examined his scar. Tears slid down her cheeks. "This is why you didn't want to see me. Why you stayed away for so long."

Romeo's throat constricted. He contorted his face to ease the pain behind his eyes, refusing to shed tears of his own. He hadn't allowed himself to cry since. . .

"Romeo, you are a soldier, a hero. You should not have let this keep us apart." She wiped at her tears then hugged him.

He held her, comforting her, hoping to dispel her anguish, especially any that he'd caused her. Finally, Romeo held her at arm's length and looked into her eyes, full into her face. He wanted her to see that he was over it. "Mama. I'm here with you now."

She smiled up at him. "Yes, and you are alive. You lived through that horrible blast that did this to you."

In his peripheral vision, Romeo saw the young woman who'd accused him of trespassing and another woman who looked familiar. Erin—he remembered meeting her once or twice a long time ago.

His mother's face brightened, and she gripped his arm while turning away. "Camille, Erin, this is my Romeo. Isn't he handsome? He's a hero, you know. He survived a terrible explosion while serving in Afghanistan."

"It's very nice to meet you." Erin stepped forward to shake his hand. "Have you eaten?"

Mama tugged on his arm. "Come inside, and we'll fix you something."

Finally, the young woman stepped forward and offered

her hand as well. "I'm Camille, Erin's niece. Welcome to our humble abode." She grinned shyly and glanced away.

Somehow Romeo sensed that her shyness had nothing to do with his scarred appearance. Lovely red curls hugged her face and fell over her shoulders. She wore a loose-fitting dress of tie-dyed bright pink, yellow, and blue. For the first time in a very long time, Romeo wanted to smile.

But he wouldn't allow himself that pleasure. Instead, he kept his expression neutral, unwilling to give any of himself away.

three

Afghanistan, a soldier, a hero. . .

Camille's breath caught in her throat. She hadn't known this about Stella's son. Why hadn't the woman shared? Or even Aunt Erin? Surely, she knew. Maybe since he'd not come to see his mother immediately after returning to the States, talking about him was too painful for her.

Camille walked behind Aunt Erin, who followed Stella and her son toward the french doors. Camille first thought she should give mother and son some time alone, but she was too mesmerized with their encounter to move or remember her manners.

She remembered them now. She rushed past the three-some, getting to the doors first.

"Please, allow me." She planned to open both doors wide, but a hand covered hers on the doorknob.

She looked up into Romeo's dark, brooding gaze.

"No, allow me," he said, his voice deep and soothing.

"Thank you." Despite the scar that began at his mutilated ear and traveled over the left side of his face and down his neck, Romeo was incredibly handsome. Camille slowly slipped her hand from under his.

Something about him both thrilled and scared her. And his name was Romeo? What were the chances?

"Whoever loved that loved not at first sight?" Shakespeare's simple question crept into her thoughts.

He held the door for Stella and Aunt Erin, and then, when Camille stood planted to the ground like one of her topiaries, Romeo extended his hand, motioning for her to enter as well.

She moved through the doors, aware of Romeo closing

them behind her. The older women had already disappeared, and Camille could hear their excited jabbering from the kitchen. She guessed she should show Romeo the way, and though she kept walking, she glanced over her shoulder to make sure he followed.

"I don't suppose you like spaghetti with sauce. That's what we had for dinner, and there's plenty left."

From behind, Romeo's laugh sounded strained. "I don't suppose you knew that my family used to run an Italian restaurant back in Indiana."

Camille chuckled. Stella had been oddly quiet about her life before she moved. "So, is that a yes or a no?"

"A home-cooked meal sounds delicious, especially if it's Italian. Mama used to make the best spaghetti."

Together, they stepped into the bright white kitchen, accented with cobalt-blue-and-white-checkered tiles on the counters. White tiles covered the floor. Sometimes the white was almost too much for Camille. Still, it was difficult to feel drab and depressed in a bright, clean kitchen.

Stella took Romeo's hand and led him to a chair she'd pulled out at the table. "Now, you sit while we serve you."

Camille squeezed Stella's shoulder. "Why don't you sit with your son? You have a lot of catching up to do. Aunt Erin and I will do the serving."

Stella's lips quivered and formed into a soft smile. She patted Camille's hand. "Thank you." She lowered herself into one of the chairs.

Camille watched Romeo study his mother. She wondered if he knew how much Stella suffered from debilitating arthritis. For the first time, Camille considered that the woman most likely suffered as well from Romeo's absence, especially since—as Stella had mentioned earlier—he'd chosen to stay away.

He was definitely an uneasy sort. Maybe time spent in the redwoods would be rest for his tired soul. Camille sensed he carried a great burden. She'd heard that beauty was only skin deep. Was the disfiguring scar on his face only skin deep? Or did it penetrate to the depths of his soul, wounding him there as well?

"Can I get you something to drink? Tea, water, milk? Peppermint tea?" Camille smiled at him.

"A glass of water would be nice, thank you."

She liked the sound of Romeo's voice. After giving him his glass, her mind began spinning with questions. She focused on assisting Aunt Erin, who'd pulled out pots and pans and was now removing the leftover spaghetti and sauce from the fridge.

"Aunt Erin, what are you doing?"

"I'm warming up dinner for Romeo."

"Just dish some out on a plate and stick it in the microwave." Camille grabbed the handle of the large pot to return it, but Aunt Erin stayed her hand.

"There's nothing like a home-cooked meal—the sounds of pans clanking, the smells of sauce boiling on the stove. A microwave can't do that." Her aunt glanced at Romeo and Stella as they talked.

Aunt Erin leaned in close and kept her voice low. "Let's give him something nice."

"Of course," Camille said, wishing she'd been as thoughtful. A soldier certainly deserved the best they could give him.

While the food reheated on the stove, Camille stood next to the table to set out a place mat, plate, and utensils for Romeo, but his arms were spread in front of him as he talked to his mother.

"Son, there's so much I haven't told you as well. . . ." Stella said. Then, as though she'd only now noticed Camille's presence, she stopped talking and stared up at her.

"Excuse me. I just need to set out your plate." She smiled down at Romeo, suddenly shy. "The food is almost ready."

"Smells like heaven." He moved his arms but didn't back

away as she spread out his place setting and utensils.

Camille was keenly aware of his nearness, feeling heat in her cheeks that had nothing to do with warming his meal. Embarrassed, she hoped neither Stella nor Aunt Erin noticed her reaction to him. "There," she said. "All done."

"And just in time, too." Aunt Erin set the large pot of spaghetti and sauce on the table. "There's plenty, Romeo. Looks like the Lord knew you were coming, because we made too much."

After dishing up a hefty plate of pasta for him, Camille and Aunt Erin made to leave the kitchen.

"Where do you think you're going?" Stella asked.

"We want to give you some privacy, that's all," Camille said.

"Nonsense. We have plenty of time for that, don't we?" Stella looked at her son as though for assurance. "I've asked Romeo to stay with us here, at least for a while."

Camille stifled a quick intake of breath and looked to her aunt, gauging her expression. Had she and Stella already discussed this? But if so, when? The things these women decided without even talking to her.

"Now, come and talk." Stella motioned for them to sit at the table. "Get to know my Romeo."

Camille and Aunt Erin obeyed and sat while Romeo stuck his first forkful in his mouth. She was curious to see his reaction, considering he'd been part of a family-run Italian restaurant.

He closed his eyes like a man who hadn't eaten in years and now savored the one thing he missed most.

Camille couldn't contain her smile. "Do you like it?" she asked.

"Mmmmmm." He opened his eyes and looked across the table at Stella. "I said it smelled like heaven, and it tastes like nothing I've ever tasted. Mama, you have perfected your recipe."

Stella smiled at Camille. "No, son. This exquisite dish belongs to Camille."

Romeo's eyes searched Camille's. She looked down at the table and played with her hands. Somewhere inside, her heart did a little jump. At that moment, she knew she'd found the inspiration she was missing. At that moment, she knew she'd paint Romeo for the Redwood Art Association's contest.

Romeo. Without his scar.

But. . .would he approve?

 près

With difficulty, Romeo tugged his gaze away from Camille's shiny red curls and shy smile. He took another bite and chewed, trying to enjoy her culinary brilliance. But with her sitting next to him and acting bashful—was she flirting with him? Or was he losing his mind?

Maybe it had been far too long since anyone had paid him any positive attention. That had to be it—he was simply reading her wrong.

After what he'd been through with his fiancée, he knew better than to fancy that Camille could be attracted to him.

He was damaged goods.

But the way she'd looked at him. He hadn't seen pity in her eyes. In fact, he'd seen—a knot formed in his throat, making it difficult to swallow—admiration.

Another bite, and he forced his thoughts to the meal rather than the company. He considered the flavors, attempting to determine the special ingredient.

"Ah, Romeo, I know that look on your face." Mama always could read him well, which was a huge part of the reason he'd stayed away from her for so long. She could read his agony— the hurt of a scarred life and a broken love.

"Yes, Mama. Basil, oregano, and garlic of course, and the rich sauce is from more tomato paste and less water." Romeo wrapped more spaghetti around his fork and held it up, drawing in the aroma as if he held a glass of fine wine.

Stella smiled. "Romeo always knows a good thing when he sees it."

"Or in this case, tastes it," Erin said.

In his peripheral vision, he could see Camille resting her chin on her hand, watching him. He wanted to ask her about her secret ingredient. If he waited, perhaps she would offer.

In coming here today, finally, he hoped to make Mama understand why he'd avoided her. Her ability to see right through him was also a strong reason to avoid looking at the lovely Camille. Already, the intriguing young woman had piqued his interest.

He told himself that his heart had healed. But perhaps the pain remained just under the surface, as though covered by a thick scab. Allowing anyone to touch it would be too painful.

Nothing he'd faced so far could be as dangerous to his soul.

After the meal, Romeo walked his mother to the front porch. She wanted to sit there awhile. She must be ready to speak to him in private. He opened the screen door for her, allowing her to shuffle outside. Maybe now she would tell him what ailed her. She could be such a stubborn and prideful woman.

She settled into a white rocking chair, Romeo into a floral-padded wicker chair, catty-corner to her.

"What's bothering you?" she asked.

A hundred things. Your health. My life. Camille. . . "I didn't figure out the secret ingredient in the spaghetti," he said.

Her laugh was worth a million dollars. "I haven't exactly been here long enough to figure it out myself, nor have I yet to catch her during the cooking."

Though Romeo hated to think of it, he knew the mother he left behind when he served in Afghanistan would have been quick to discover Camille's ingredient even if she had to be devious about it. He dreaded asking her the next question.

"Mama, what is going on?" *Are you sick?* "Why did you sell the family business and move here?" His heart ached at the thought for too many reasons—he had nowhere to call home now. He had no life—the restaurant was gone. He'd counted on it being there when he got back. If only he'd counted the cost before he left. He'd lost so much.

He hoped he wouldn't have to drag the answer out of her.

When she sighed, he heard in her a weaker soul than he remembered.

"I'll answer you, if you'll answer one of my questions."

Here it comes. She wanted to know why he hadn't allowed her to visit him in the hospital as he endured corrective surgery after surgery. Finally he'd said enough was enough. He would never be the same no matter how many surgeries.

"Why did you break off your engagement?"

four

The next morning, Camille climbed the stairs to the attic and covered the yawn that escaped. She'd gotten no rest last night, because she'd found her inspiration for a new painting. But how did she ask Romeo if she could paint him without his scar? She hardly knew the man. The subject would be awkward at best.

That is, if she could find the nerve to bring it up. She blew out a breath and tugged her stubborn hair back into a clip. She practically stumbled through the attic door, covering yet another yawn with the back of her hand. How was she going to get any work done today?

Camille stopped midstride. Someone stood in the room.

Romeo? "What—what are you doing here?" *The nerve!* But then, maybe he'd come to see her. Her insides grew warm.

"I'm sorry." He shrugged. "I didn't mean to startle you." Romeo just stood there and stared at her with those big, dark eyes, uninhibited despite his scar.

Should she ask him about painting his portrait now? Or. . . No. She felt entirely too uncomfortable under his gaze. "No problem." She smiled and walked past him to her desk. "It's not every day I find a man in my office, that's all."

Romeo turned as she swept by. She could sense him watching her every move. Could she have made a mistake, thinking he was her inspiration? She wasn't sure she would grow accustomed to his intensity.

"I think I've offended you. It wasn't my intention to barge into an empty office. I heard a noise and thought you were here already."

She sat in the swivel chair next to her desk. While her

computer booted up, she stole a glance his way. "You wanted to talk to me, then?"

"Yes. To apologize for scaring you last night."

"Oh, I wasn't scared."

"The way you threatened me, I could have sworn you thought I was a member of a motorcycle gang who had come to kidnap someone," he said, half of his face smiling. Somehow, she knew his half smile had nothing to do with his scarred muscles.

But threatened him? Warmth suffused her neck. "If you really wanted to hurt me, my threats wouldn't have done a thing."

"You standing there like a tie-dyed fairy—you were the picture of resistance." Again, the partial grin. "It was a brave stand."

A brave stand? "That was nothing compared with what you've seen in battles, I'm sure." Ugh. She should have chosen her words better. Camille wanted to curl up and hide in one of her handbags.

He didn't even flinch. "I hope you never have to see what I've seen."

Wasn't he sensitive about his appearance? Another thing to admire about him. Or, maybe he was good at hiding his emotions, too.

All this time, he'd remained like a bronze statue in the middle of her room, not far from her easel.

Then suddenly the sculpture sprang to life and approached the paintings on her wall. Silent and contemplative, he moved around the attic as though it were a museum containing valuable paintings by an artist long dead.

Camille held her breath. She longed to know what he thought of her art, her work. Why was his approval so important to her?

"Oh, there you are," Stella said, peeking around the door. She encouraged it all the way open and smiled at her son.

"Breakfast is ready and waiting in the kitchen."

Camille exhaled while Aunt Erin breezed through the door behind Stella, holding a steaming cup. "Thought you might like some coffee."

She set the dark brew on Camille's desk and swiped her hand down her apron. This morning, Camille's Attic had become a busy airport terminal.

"Yes, thank you." She smiled at her aunt. "I have to deliver bags this morning, so I won't be down for breakfast."

Aunt Erin had that pleased look on her face. She was glad Camille was finally going to deliver her latest bags to local vendors.

"You can't sell them if they're not in the stores." Her aunt's mantra needled her.

Stella only had eyes for Romeo, but it seemed, this morning at least, he only had eyes for Camille. Concern edged his gaze. "You go ahead, Mama. I'll be right down."

Stella pursed her lips and glanced at Camille. "Well, all right. If you're sure."

"I'm sure."

The two older women left the attic. This could be Camille's chance to ask Romeo about the painting, but something squeezed her throat.

Air. She had to get air. Camille rose from the chair and opened the windows on both sides of the attic. The morning breeze drifted through, lifting her spirits and her unruly hair from its clip.

&

Romeo touched one of the large bags resting on a shelf and ran his finger down the colorful cloth, accented with beads and a wooden handle. Stacks of cloth sat in the corner next to what looked like a sewing machine on steroids. There was no doubt about Camille's talent. And considering the large canvas on the easel, she was multitalented, too.

In addition to that, her spaghetti sauce was divine. He

angled a glance her way, watching her inhale the cool morning air. He'd wanted to see Camille and apologize.

But there was more to it than that.

Yesterday he'd seen something in her eyes that wasn't pity, and he craved to see it again. But she was avoiding his eyes now—maybe her lack of pity was short lived. Still, he wished he knew her better. She seemed like the sort of person he'd like to talk to, confide in.

That was a dangerous path to travel—he'd resigned himself to a life without love, and he could see that being in the same house with Camille would drive him nuts in keeping his resolve.

She'd already stirred something in him he'd long put to rest. Or at least he'd thought he had. But she'd awakened it without even trying.

Finally, Camille turned away from the window. Her red curls appeared to have enjoyed riding the wind. He allowed himself a smile.

"What?" Color crept over her cheeks. She began shoving her hair back in its pins.

He fought back the urge to approach her and remove all those clips and pins, allowing her hair the freedom it apparently desired.

Instead, he traced the edges of the canvas and grinned, hoping she'd relax a little—like she had last night. "Who made the large, black stroke across this painting of a redwood tree? Surely you didn't do that."

Camille drew in a breath and rushed to the painting. She pulled a large cloth over to hide it, shaking her head. "I'm sorry you had to see that."

"But why be sorry? It was almost a perfect likeness of that photograph on the table. You've got a lot of talent."

"I meant I'm sorry you had to see the method I use to kill paintings."

Romeo chuckled. "Oh, is that what you call it?" She was a strange bird, but he liked her.

"I needed to rid myself from feeling obligated to it. It was a painting completely devoid of inspiration or emotion. If you've ever painted, you know how difficult it can be to capture the majesty of God's creation on canvas."

"I guess I'm not a good judge, then, because the painting was one of the best I've seen."

"You really think so?" Her eyes, the color of the Mediterranean, searched his.

"I really think so."

"You're not just saying that because you want me to tell you my secret ingredient to the spaghetti sauce?"

Romeo rolled his head back in laughter. "That hadn't even occurred to me. But would it work?"

"No. It will take a lot more than that."

As she looked up at him, this time she didn't flinch under his gaze. He studied the delicate structure of her face and her creamy skin, dotted with a few freckles across the nose. And all the while he studied her, she did the same to him—her eyes traveling the length of the good side of his face and then studying his scar as though pained that he'd suffered. But in no way did he sense that she was repulsed at the sight of him.

Camille lifted her hand and held it inches from the scar.

He knew she wanted to touch it. The very idea ripped through him, tearing him—he wanted desperately for someone to care deeply about him, to go beyond his scar. But at the same time, her gesture renewed the pain all over again.

The pain of losing the woman he loved.

"Romeo," she whispered. "There's something I'd like to—"

"Romeo," Stella snapped, standing in the doorway.

Her voice jarred him from the irrational place Camille's magic had taken him.

"What are you doing?" she asked, her tone antagonistic. "I thought you were coming down to breakfast. Your bacon is getting cold. Don't make me climb these stairs looking for you again."

He stared at his mother. So did Camille. Mama looked accusingly at them, and at that moment, he realized how close together they were standing. Mama suspected something was going on, and she didn't like it.

Oh boy.

five

After Stella left the room, Camille stepped away from Romeo and toyed with a few paintbrushes. She'd never heard Stella speak in that tone before. With his frown, Romeo seemed equally stunned. How would he respond to his mother? What had happened to his father? There was so much about him Camille wanted to know. She'd been on the verge of asking him if she could paint him, but should she broach the subject of his portrait so soon? If she wanted his consent, timing would be important. She needed to gain his trust.

"What were you going to ask?" The troubled look on his face vanished.

"Oh, it was nothing, really." She twirled the paintbrush, a nervous laugh escaping.

"Don't let my mother worry you." He took the paintbrush from her hands and stuck it back in the jar. "It feels good, actually."

She looked him in the eye, trying not to fidget. "What feels good?"

"Her bossing me around like I'm a boy makes me feel at home, like things used to be."

Camille couldn't help herself. "But you're not a boy, Romeo. You're a grown man. A hero." Too late, she bit her tongue. She had no business questioning his relationship with his mother.

He quirked a brow. "And I'm man enough to not react like a child. I want to honor my mother. For the little while that I'm here, I should give her that at least, don't you think?"

For the little while that he was here?

Romeo left Camille's side and headed for the door. Though he walked with relaxed confidence, Camille worried that she had offended him.

When his hand gripped the doorknob, Camille started to follow. "Romeo, wait."

He paused, holding the doorknob. Reaching him, she pressed her fingers to his arm. He stiffened, and Camille instantly dropped her hand to her side.

He turned to face her, his expression troubled. "Well?" he asked. Her throat constricted, making her second-guess herself. "I need to deliver handbags this morning. Would you like to tag along and carry some boxes for me?"

Oh, that was weak. She wanted to gag.

"Is that what you were you going to ask me before my mother interrupted?"

"Yes. I thought I could show you around town at the same time."

"I'd like that, but right after I eat breakfast. Care to join me?"

After that look Stella gave her? Camille shook her head. "I need to get the bags ready for delivery."

He nodded and left. Camille closed the door and leaned against it, allowing her gaze to scan the disorganization that was her attic office. As she made her way across the floor, she could feel the difference in the room.

Romeo had been here, filling her attic with his presence, and now the room would never be the same. The man had ignited her muse, and if she could harness the inspiration, she believed with all her heart she might have a chance to win the art contest.

And winning would give her the power to change her life forever.

ও৯

"Eat, Romeo, eat," Mama encouraged him, shoving a plateful of pancakes and another plate of bacon and eggs in front of him.

Romeo poured syrup over the pancakes while he listened to Mama chatter with Erin. If he busied himself eating, he wouldn't be expected to talk or answer questions. He hated seeing Mama's painful movements yesterday. She told him it was rheumatoid arthritis, but he could tell she was having a good day today. He wondered if he was the reason.

Now he could see why she'd moved in with her longtime friend. They were comfortable with each other and a good fit.

But Erin's niece, Camille? Not such a good fit. At least what little he knew about her.

"And now that my Romeo is here. . ." Mama patted his hand.

He swallowed a bite of bacon, acknowledging that she'd now turned her attention to him.

"But you're not a boy, Romeo. You're a grown man. . . ."

Camille's words tumbled over his thoughts. He had told Camille that he enjoyed the feelings of normalcy—in fact, he longed for them. But his relationship with Mama was slipping back into what it was in the past. He saw now what he feared—coming home wouldn't be that easy. He could never go back to the way life was before. He had the scars to prove it.

Mama could smother him if he let her, even though he'd been on his own for years.

"I thought we could move that old trunk out of the storage room outside," Mama said. "And there's some other furniture in my bedroom I need resituated. Plus, we probably should paint the house, don't you think, Erin? Oh, we have got so much to talk about, Romeo. I don't even know where to start."

Romeo smiled around a mouthful of eggs. *Lord, help me be a good son.* "Maybe another day. I've already agreed to help Camille today."

Her mouth pursed into a tight circle. "Help Camille? What on earth could she need help with?"

Erin slipped into a kitchen chair and held a cup of coffee. "She's busy with her handbags this morning, or at least she led me to believe she would be working on building her business. She needs a Plan B in case she doesn't win that contest."

The way Erin said the words made Romeo wonder if the business had been Camille's idea or Erin's. "I can help her carry the boxes, and she's going to show me around town."

Mama seemed to relax, if only a little. "Oh well, that's good then. Someone needs to show you around."

Romeo stifled a heavy sigh by downing a cup of coffee. He would need to have a talk with Mama sooner rather than later. And here he'd been concerned about her reaction to his scar. She acted as though he hadn't just spent the last few years in the army, surviving an IED blast and recovering from his injuries. "I'll see you later today then." He slid from the chair and pushed it forward. "Ladies."

He found Camille stumbling down the stairs, loaded down with handbags.

"Here, let me help you with that." He rushed to her side before she could overstep and miss the last two steps.

"Oh, thank goodness," she said. "I guess I took too many of these."

Romeo wasn't exactly sure how to grab them but gathered as many handles as he could. "I thought you were boxing these."

"Some of them are boxed. These are what's left."

"You've been busy."

Erin appeared in the foyer. "Let me get the door for you."

The door opened wide. Romeo carried the bags through, leading Camille. "Sorry that we can't take my ride," he said.

Camille chuckled. "I didn't realize you rode a motorcycle. I'm surprised I didn't hear you drive up."

She led the way over to her Honda Accord. "I'm afraid my car doesn't hold that much, either, but I only have four shops

I deliver to locally."

Romeo helped her tuck the remainder of the bags in the backseat of her car. Boxes took up the trunk. "So you're delivering these to the shop owners who are expecting you?"

"Yep," she said and climbed into the driver's seat.

Romeo opened the door and sat in the passenger's seat next to her. The car was small, and he felt too close to Camille. Suddenly he wondered what he was doing by riding along. He felt exposed. On his motorcycle, he wore his helmet, and no one could see his face.

Camille stopped at a four-way stop and waited for the car on the right to go first. The driver's gaze seemed to linger longer than necessary. Was she looking at Romeo? He tensed, wrestling with his self-consciousness. Enough time had passed—why couldn't he get over it? What was the matter with him?

"Redbrook is a small tourist town, and I have several friends who own shops. They always welcome my creations, whether paintings or these handbags." She turned left and accelerated.

"You're very talented. Are the handbags how you support yourself? I mean, are they your business?"

She sent a cursory grin his way and tugged a loose red curl behind her ear. "Not hardly, though I'm trying to build the business. I also teach art classes. Plus, I live with my aunt, and that helps us both financially."

He wondered about his mother's financial arrangement with them. "And the handbags were your aunt's idea?"

She grinned. "You're very perceptive. She had a sewing machine that I could use. Plus, I enjoy being creative. It's fun."

During the remainder of the short drive, Camille talked about the little town that was dubbed a "Victorian village," nestled between the redwood forests. She drove downtown and parked her car at the curb. It seemed they'd stepped into the last century, the shops accented with quaint porches and painted in every possible earth tone.

She got out and put coins in the parking meter. Romeo climbed from the car and waited for Camille's instructions. She opened the door to the backseat and pulled out a few bags, and Romeo did the same on the other side.

They slammed the doors shut, and she looked over at him. "You ready?"

He nodded, but from his point of view, the question was loaded. No, he was definitely not prepared to meet the people of this town, wearing a smile and a friendly manner, pretending not to notice the stares.

He hadn't completely thought this trip through. From the sound of it, he would have to interact with a lot of people today. And all this because he decided it was time to allow his mother to see what her handsome Romeo had become.

He couldn't let Camille down, though—not after he'd offered to help. He followed her into a store called Mary's Curios. A bell dinged, announcing their presence.

A woman in her late forties appeared from the back corner, between various knickknacks and a clothing rack. A few leather purses lined the top of the rack.

"Ah, there you are. I wondered when you'd drop off your bags again. Business is about to pick up in the next few weeks with the art festival." The woman offered a genuine smile then took some of the bags from Camille. "How are you doing? I've missed you."

Camille smiled in return and glanced at Romeo. "I'm swamped as usual."

When the shop owner noticed Romeo, she quickly averted her gaze from his scar to his eyes. "Who is your friend, Camille?"

"Remember meeting Stella, who lives with us now? This is her son, Romeo." Camille smiled at him. "Romeo, meet Mary."

"It's a pleasure," he said. He avoided Mary's uncomfortable gaze and the obvious questions behind her eyes.

Mary nodded and moved her attention to Camille. "What are you painting for the contest?"

Camille sighed. "It's a surprise."

"Oh, you. Maybe you'll share something about it on that Shakespeare blog of yours."

Shakespeare blog? Camille's many layers intrigued Romeo.

While Mary and Camille discussed business and arranged the handbags, Romeo explored the store. When he and Camille were alone, he'd ask her about the contest and the blog.

A figurine drew his attention.

He lifted it from its perch for closer examination. He'd never seen one like it—a woman hovered over a fallen soldier.

Bitterness soured his stomach and sent an ache through his heart.

Through shelving laid heavy with art, decor, and clothing, Romeo caught a glimpse of Camille.

Meeting her brought his doubts to the surface. They went much deeper than his appearance. Dread sifted through him at the thought of finding love, of having to face the pain of his past—a pain caused by his own impulsiveness.

six

Camille meandered among the easels, glancing at the oil paintings as her art students busied themselves adding texture and depth to their chosen landscapes. She paused behind Matt, one of her longtime students, and hovered at his shoulder to study the brook gently washing over pebbles, hugged by giant ferns.

In his late twenties, he was quite the artist. She loved his work but didn't want to emphasize just how much in front of the others. "Good, Matt. You've really captured the details. I can practically hear the brook."

"I hoped you'd like it." He kept his attention on his brushstrokes.

"I do." In fact, she loved it. If she hung it on the wall in her room it would soothe her to sleep as easily as a recording of relaxing sounds. But she couldn't possibly sleep tonight without beginning her own painting. Inspiration infused her, though she hadn't braved the topic with Romeo yet.

"I know how much you love the redwoods," he said, tossing a smile her way.

His gaze lingered a few seconds too long for comfort. She nodded and moved down the aisle to another student.

"And how's yours coming along, sweet Lorraine?" Camille loved the elderly woman who was working to complete her bucket list.

"I think I need a little more beach and a little less ocean." Lorraine chuckled.

One of the fluorescent lights flickered and went partially dark. Again. Camille sighed. She taught evening classes in the back of an art supply store. Her students bought their supplies from the store, so the owners didn't require Camille to pay rent. It was a mutually beneficial agreement, but the lighting was atrocious. One day she hoped to teach a workshop outside in the sunlight.

She left Lorraine's side and strolled to the front of the class. "I think that about does it for tonight. Go ahead and clean up your work center, and I'll see you next week."

After the students straightened the room and left, Camille shut off the lights and stepped outside to lock the door. At eight thirty, it was nearly dark, but in a few weeks the sun would offer up ample light at this hour. And in a few weeks, she reminded herself, the art festival would take over the town. She couldn't wait any longer to begin her painting of Romeo.

Three days had passed since his arrival, and somehow Stella had managed to keep him busy, moving furniture around, painting her room, and even making plans for him to paint the house.

Camille walked around the side of the building to the parking lot in front. A motorcycle rumbled nearby, and the rider parked next to her car.

Her breath caught in her throat. Romeo.

This time, instead of his black leather biker pants, he wore blue jeans and a button-down shirt under his leather jacket. He tugged off his helmet and set it on his thigh. When he smiled at her, pleasant feelings twirled like dandelions in her stomach.

She smiled back at him while she walked to her car. "What are you doing here?"

"Want to go for a ride?"

His question stunned her, but she recovered and giggled. She'd never been on a motorcycle in her life.

"I'm afraid my aunt Erin would have a fit," she said, unlocking her car door and tossing in her handbag.

Romeo quirked a brow at her. "How old are you again?"

Huffing a laugh, Camille hung her head. "You're referring to my taunt the other day, that you're a grown man, aren't you?"

He laughed. "If you could call it that."

She seriously needed to get started on her painting tonight, especially while the muse called her. But what could it hurt to spend more time with her inspiration? Besides, she'd missed spending some time alone with him like they'd done the day she showed him around town.

Camille locked her car and turned around to find him watching her. *What are you thinking behind those dark eyes of yours, Romeo?*

He handed her another helmet, which she hadn't noticed before, and helped her to secure it.

"You never did answer my question. What are you doing here?" She tucked her hair into the helmet.

"I was in the neighborhood." He fastened the strap under her chin. His cologne enveloped her, making her a little light headed. When he was done, she smiled at him. He climbed onto the seat and turned the ignition on.

Camille wasn't exactly sure what to do next and hesitated until Romeo looked at her.

"Are you getting on or what? Make sure you hold on tight."

"Are you saying you want me to hold on to you?"

"If you don't want to fall off, then yes, you should hold on to me," he said, his voice muffled inside the helmet. Still, she could hear laughter in his voice.

Camille swung her leg over to straddle the motorcycle then wrapped her arms snugly around Romeo's waist. She could feel his strong back. She'd never been to this place before. It was. . .

Heaven.

ॐ

Laughing and loving the way Camille had clung to him, the way she was making him feel, Romeo followed her into the house. After a short ride on his motorcycle, he'd taken her back to her car and followed her home.

Stepping into the foyer after her, he closed the door. Assuming no one would be leaving the house since it was well after nine, he locked everything up.

Camille dropped one of her signature handbags—this one of blue denim and canvas—into a chair, then leaned against the wall, a casual grin on her face as she played with her keys. Her red curls fell over her shoulders in a tangled mess. Right now, she reminded him of a sprite. She fit in perfectly with her surroundings—the garden in front and the landscape edged by redwood forest on one side, the low mountain range on the other.

"So, what's next for you, Romeo?"

He couldn't help but smile. She really knew how to get right to the crux of things.

Erin and Mama came scurrying from the kitchen. Any other time he would have resented their interruption. But at the moment, he welcomed it.

"Camille, where have you been?" Erin asked. When she saw Romeo, her eyes lit up, though her face still wore an expression of disapproval. "I've been worried about you."

Mama moved from behind Erin, a frown on her lips. "Am I to understand that you two have spent the evening together?"

"I'm sorry I didn't call." Camille hugged her aunt. "My class ended a little late, and then Romeo took me for a ride."

Aunt Erin gasped. "You mean on his motorcycle?"

"Yes," Camille said with amusement. "It was exhilarating. You really should try it sometime."

Erin gasped and followed Camille into the kitchen. "What were you thinking? You could have been killed."

Camille's soft answer escaped Romeo as Mama's stare bored into him. "How could you, Romeo?"

He began to climb the stairs to the guest room. "What are you talking about?"

She followed him up the stairs. "You were engaged to

a wonderful girl. Now you're cavorting around town with Camille?"

"I was engaged, Mama. *Was* being the operative word." Romeo opened the door to the guest room and entered, knowing full well that Mama would follow.

He tugged off his jacket, remembering his statement to Camille that it felt good for his mother to treat him like she used to. Now his words were coming back to bite him.

"Romeo, it broke my heart when you left. Then when your father died. . ." She gripped the post of the bed and lowered herself to sit. "And I've hoped and prayed for you to return so you could run the business again."

"You sold that, remember?" He tossed his jacket on the bed and squashed the concern squeezing his heart. Mama couldn't be losing her memory.

Unwelcome images flooded him. Had she forgotten why he'd left the family business and enlisted? That move had been a bold one on his part—an impulsive decision that cost him everything.

Mama took his hand in hers. "You can build the business again, Romeo. Right here in this little town. I believe in you."

"I only wanted to see you, to make sure you were all right. I hadn't planned on staying that long." Kent was holding a job for Romeo, hoping for help with his motorcycle business. Romeo could be a mechanic, working in the back. He'd never have to see anyone—or let anyone see him. With no other prospects, he'd thought it was his best choice. Now his future—his life—seemed more uncertain than ever.

"Son, it's time to stop running. You can build a life here, have a family."

A family? He'd left that idea behind with his fiancée—that is, until Camille. Romeo removed his hand from Mama's grip and crossed his arms. "Can I ask you, then, what have you got against Camille?"

His question seemed to energize Mama, like it gave her

hope that he was considering her proposal. "She's flighty, for one thing." Mama rose from the bed and waved her hands in the air. "And for another, she's making plans to leave. That's why Erin asked me to move here and stay, because she knew I needed a place, and Camille was trying to move out."

Despite Romeo's own plans to leave, the news threw him. "Leaving? Where's she going?"

"I just don't want to see you get hurt again." Mama squeezed his cheek, avoiding the scarred side and his question, then left the room.

The bed squeaked when Romeo sat down. So, Camille was leaving. Why should Romeo care one way or the other, since he was leaving, too? No plans to stay. None.

Being with her tonight, he'd almost forgotten about his scar. He touched the mutilated skin on his face. And yet he knew the dangers. Spending time with her could lead to the very pain he wanted to avoid. Mama had seen that as well, and while she tried to warn him, she also wanted to keep him close to her.

He couldn't blame her for that. The woman had lost two sons and a husband, and now she might lose her son again.

"What's next for you, Romeo?" Camille's words burned inside him.

Romeo tugged his leather jacket back on and bounded down the stairs. He needed to feel the wind on his face and the road beneath him.

≈

Camille flipped on the bedside lamp and slid under the covers. She grabbed the little book containing a few of Shakespeare's plays from the table and looked for her place, but her thoughts were too distracted.

After Romeo had brought her home, she'd grabbed a glass of milk in the kitchen and reassured Aunt Erin that she was safe on Romeo's motorcycle. It wouldn't do to admit to her aunt that she'd been terrified at first herself.

In the quiet of her bedroom a chuckle escaped her as she considered just why she'd agreed to a ride with Romeo. He was excitement, adventure, and mystery wrapped up in a leather package, and tonight he'd painted the landscape of her rather boring life with new, vibrant colors. He'd added texture, and if he stayed long enough, she could even see him putting depth into her soul.

Oh girl, what are you thinking? She sank down a little in her bed, thumbing through the pages of Shakespeare. Tonight, Romeo had taken her on the ride of her life. Even in the dimming light of day, she loved how the hills had looked from the seat of his motorcycle. He thrilled her, and yet he was dangerous—Romeo's scars went much deeper than his face.

Earlier, upon heading to her bedroom, she'd passed his room and overheard a heated discussion with his mother— not so much the words, but the tones. Stella sounded overwrought, and Romeo sounded. . .well, cold.

Or at least colder to Stella than Camille had heard so far, and he claimed to want to honor his mother. A few minutes later, she'd heard the rumble of his motorcycle grow distant. It pained her to think that he'd been so upset that he left.

Camille hoped Stella wouldn't drive Romeo away for good.

seven

Too excited to sleep any longer, Camille rose at six thirty and turned her alarm off before it buzzed at seven. Aunt Erin would already be downstairs reading the paper. Camille didn't feel like discussing the reason for her enthusiasm this morning, but she needed coffee.

After tugging on sweats to go with the T-shirt she slept in, she crept past Romeo's room. She recalled that he had left on his motorcycle late last night. She hadn't heard him return. Descending the stairs, she frowned, hoping she wouldn't have to face Stella this morning.

The discord between Romeo and his mother left Camille with a lingering bad feeling, due in part, she was sure, to fuzzy but disturbing dreams. Still, she was anxious to begin the painting she hoped would land her the art scholarship.

At the bottom of the stairs, she paused to listen. She couldn't hear any voices. She exhaled and relaxed a little as she made her way into the kitchen. Through the dining room window, she could see Aunt Erin and Stella standing on the deck outside, holding coffee and talking, pointing to something in the yard. Probably something Stella wanted Romeo to do.

Camille poured a large mug of coffee, added all the necessary fillers, and headed to her attic office. Finally, she could answer the empty canvas's call. She selected all the paints and brushes. The one thing she was missing was the usual photograph she worked from. But that wouldn't do this time.

She hadn't asked Romeo's permission to paint him. She decided she would undertake a tribute to him, so it would need to be a surprise. Romeo was a hero, and she hoped he would feel honored.

Quick-drying colors would work best for the background. Then she could sketch in the outline of Romeo's face and begin the detail work. A little niggling doubt crept in— had she convinced herself she was doing the right thing because this was what she wanted to do? Or would Romeo disapprove? Would she hurt him?

She sighed and fought to hang on to the inspiration that would carry her through. She'd simply guard the painting closely and reveal it at the right moment. She didn't have time to wait for the opportunity to ask Romeo.

After painting the background, Camille stood back and examined the canvas. She needed to let her creative juices brew a little before starting the rest, so she filled out the entry paperwork for the art show.

She'd need to deliver this personally today, since she was close to the deadline for entry. Camille stuffed the application in an envelope and put it in her purse while she booted up her computer. She wanted to post some thoughts on her blog today about last night's reading before they left her entirely.

After writing the post, she began skimming comments to her previous posts. The mysterious Don John had commented several times more.

Camille read the last post and swallowed.

I've seen you around town, carrying your pretty handbags. You're beautiful.

Not so unusual. Several of her blog readers lived in town. Mary had mentioned the blog the other day when Camille had delivered her bags. But his comment left her feeling uneasy. She slid her hand to her throat.

Uncertain what to think, Camille shut down her computer and pushed back from the desk. Time had slipped away from her—it was already late morning. After chnging clothes, she grabbed her purse and keys and bounded down the stairs. She headed out the back door to find Aunt Erin planting more petunias while Stella sat in a lawn chair like she was directing a movie.

"Morning, Camille." Aunt Erin scrunched her nose when she looked up from the dark earth. "Going somewhere?"

"I need some fresh air and thought I'd take a hike."

"To the tree?" Aunt Erin asked.

"In the park?" Stella asked.

Camille chuckled. "Yes. It helps me clear my head. I'll be back later."

Too bad Stella didn't get around that well. Camille suspected the woman would adore the trees as much as she did. Who wouldn't?

After delivering her application, she took the short drive to the redwoods and parked. Stepping from her car, she locked it and inhaled the scent of the forest—an earthy mix of moss, pine needles, and flowers.

In the parking lot, she stared up at the lofty redwoods standing at the foot of the trailhead, sentries guarding the forest's entrance. Though the morning was cool, things would warm up quickly, and she zipped her light jacket.

The forest beckoned, and she answered, leaving behind her car, the parking lot, and civilization. She imagined herself somewhere far away. Easy to do as the scenery transformed around her.

This is more like it. Hiking along the trail always cleared her head and infused her with peace. Where else in the world could she admire the majesty of these primeval trees?

Thank You, Lord. Your majesty surrounds me on every side. How could she worry when God had thought about every detail? Still, He'd given men the ability to choose—Camille supposed that's where her concerns set in. Was she making the right choices?

A few yards away, she spotted a fairy ring—a cluster of redwoods that grew around the stump of a dead giant. The three child trees clung to their mother long deceased, giving

Camille the perfect place to climb into the middle where their trunks joined together. When she looked straight up, the tops of the trees formed a circle with the sky at the center.

Resting her back against the rough bark of one of the giants, she drew in a breath of mist-laden air and savored the mossy smell.

Why had she allowed the blog comment to rattle her? She had overreacted, and yet. . . The idea of someone watching her, someone who'd failed to identify himself, disturbed her.

A soft breeze rustled through the trees yet didn't quite reach her through the protective canopy. Camille loved its gentle whisper, allowing it to cascade over her and sweep her anxiety away.

Somewhere in the distance, footfalls padded the trail, soft and muted. Another hiker along this branch of trails wasn't unusual. But for the first time, unease broke the peace that always enveloped Camille in the redwoods.

❧

Romeo stood in the midst of a copse of giant trees, wearing jeans and his biker boots. His gaze followed the huge trunks until he was looking straight up. He guessed they reached over two hundred feet, maybe three hundred. After looking back to the well-worn trail, he continued his hike. He could easily understand why Camille loved this place so much, or so her aunt had claimed when she told him about Camille's morning jaunt on the redwood trail. Erin said Camille often hiked here, looking for inspiration for her art.

After seeing her parked car, Romeo thought she would be as easy to find, though he hoped he wouldn't interrupt her or cause her to lose the flash of an idea.

He hiked the trail for about a quarter of a mile.

There, in the fused base of three trees, Camille leaned against one of them, dwarfed by their size. Romeo paused to soak in the picture. If only he, too, were an artist.

But her expression showed anything but inspiration—in fact, she frowned and leaned forward as though watching and listening. He might second-guess his decision to interrupt her privacy, except for the apprehension on her face. Maybe he'd come at the right time. He took a step, and something crunched under his foot.

Camille's eyes flashed his direction, then her expression softened as she smiled. "Romeo!" She scrambled from the tree.

Encouraged by her enthusiasm, Romeo pushed forward to meet her halfway. She rushed to him as though she would throw her arms around him then stopped herself.

He gripped her arms. "Is everything all right?"

"Of course." She shrugged out of his clutch. "Why would you ask that?"

"Because you looked worried. Scared."

"You saw me? Why didn't you say something instead of just standing there?"

"You're changing the subject."

"Am not."

Romeo sighed. She wasn't going to tell him. "I'd rather know the answer to this question than the secret ingredient to your spaghetti sauce."

"How did you find me?"

"What makes you think I was looking?" He tried to infuse his question with a teasing tone. "Maybe I wanted to go for a walk in the park the same as you."

"I'm glad you're here." She angled her head and smiled.

An awkward silence grew between them.

Camille glanced down. "Oh look, it's a banana slug." She crouched to get a closer look. Romeo did the same. "I wouldn't even have seen it if you hadn't pointed it out. It's camouflaged."

"They're one of the world's biggest slugs."

"Makes sense that they're in this forest, then." He swallowed. Their faces were inches apart.

Camille eyed him. "Since you're here, would you like to take a walk with me?"

"Sure." Romeo kept pace beside her where the trail allowed, hiking in comfortable silence along the worn path.

"So, did you really come here for a walk, or did my aunt tell you where to find me?" Camille asked, finally breaking the quiet.

"That sounds like a trick question to me." Romeo chuckled. "Your aunt told me you would be here."

"Why were you looking?"

"Do I need a reason?" He wanted to ask her thoughts about him starting a business in town. If he stayed, would she stay, too? He frowned, unsure if he should broach the topic yet. He wasn't even sure if Camille really had plans to leave. That could be a story Mama had concocted for her own benefit. She wasn't exactly thrilled about Romeo's interest in Camille.

Camille grinned as though his response pleased her.

He liked that.

"No, you don't need a reason." She sent him a wry smile and hopped over a crumbling log that lay across the trail. "I heard you drive off on your motorcycle last night after everyone was in bed. What was that all about?"

Romeo wasn't sure he wanted to ruin his time with Camille by dumping all his baggage on her. "I'd rather you tell me what you know about these trees."

Her face lit up. "To tell you the truth, I figured your mother would have you working again today. So I was a little surprised at seeing you here, but if you really want to know about the trees. . ."

She paused midstride and turned just as Romeo took a step. He bumped into her, nearly knocking her off her feet. He grabbed her elbow to steady her.

Camille looked up into his face, straight into his eyes as though he didn't even have a scar. He saw no focused effort to keep her gaze from drifting to the mangled part of his face, as he'd seen in the eyes of so many others.

His heart ached.

His face near hers, her breathing grew shallow.

Romeo's throat constricted, and he almost forgot what he was about to say before they collided. "Yes, I really want to know. . ." *about you, Camille.*

eight

Camille's face was so close to Romeo that his words feathered softly against her cheeks. Again the thrill of mystery and danger roared through her. She closed her eyes and swallowed, wondering what it would be like to kiss this man, to feel his strength embrace her. At the moment, she could hardly think of anything else.

Romeo was an attractive man, whatever others thought. She sensed there was much more to him, too, than his attractiveness. God looked at the heart, as should she—and drawn to Romeo, she wanted to know his heart. But how did one learn these things?

Time. It would take time.

Camille wasn't certain she had the time she needed, but she couldn't rush things, either. Just like the ancient redwoods. They stood magnificent and beautiful, heedless to the rush of life around them as they took centuries to grow.

Still, a redwood seedling knew its path. Camille could not say the same for herself. She shoved all her doubts about the future to a dark corner of her mind. She forced herself to smile. "You might want to change your mind about letting me be your tour guide. I happen to know a lot about these trees."

Romeo quirked a brow. "I had a hunch you might."

She took a step back, considering her next words. "Then there's nothing that would give me more pleasure." Camille couldn't recall when she'd ever been given the chance to share her love for the redwoods with anyone. His request filled her with delight, flooding her being, inspiring her once again. "For starters, these ancient trees were living when the

Romans ruled the world, some of them alive when Christ walked the earth."

"That's amazing," Romeo said. His gaze took on a thoughtful look.

"Still, nobody really knows how old the biggest ones are. They'd have to drill inside to count the growth rings." Camille smiled as an idea wormed into her thoughts. "Come on. There's something I want to show you." In her excitement, she almost ran along the trail. After a glance back, she laughed at the confused look on Romeo's face. He must think she was crazy. She arrived at the bend in the trail and pointed. "See over there?"

Romeo's gaze followed. His eyes widened. "That's it! That's the tree in your photograph—the one you painted."

"The very same." Camille started toward it. "I think it's one of the taller ones—over three hundred and fifty feet tall. But of course, I'm guessing. I can't be sure."

"Hey, aren't you supposed to stay on the trail?"

"Yeah, that's one of those guidelines. Not necessarily a rule." She pushed through the ferns.

Romeo's boots crunched on the needles behind her. "I suppose you think that since you're an artist, you're given license to trample the forest."

"Do you see any trampling going on here?" She raised an eyebrow at him.

"I don't suppose you can trespass in a forest where you belong." Romeo's gaze showed only appreciation.

She grinned. Earlier he had called her a sprite.

Watching Romeo lean against her favorite of all the redwoods in the forest, she wished she'd brought her camera.

He gazed at the canopy of leaves above him. "It's not difficult to understand why you love these gentle giants."

"Only the extremely large ones are called giants, and the very biggest, titans." Camille strolled over to lean next to him. "I know about the redwoods, but I know nothing about you, Romeo."

Was it her imagination, or did he sag against the tree? He closed his eyes.

Camille stared at the ground, sorry that she had somehow destroyed the ambiance. But now that she had, she might as well push forward. . . .

"What do you want to know?" he asked, shoving himself away from the tree.

Camille suspected he liked to move around when he was troubled, whether pacing or driving off on his motorcycle. She followed him back to the trail, glad that time seemed to stand still in the redwoods. She could stay here forever with Romeo, if that's how long it took to learn about him.

"Have you ever been in love?" She blurted the question.

Romeo's shoulders tensed as he stepped onto the trail in front of her. "Yes."

Camille hopped over a small fern and followed him. Her heart ached at his answer. Was he still in love? How could she ask him, if he were unwilling to elaborate? She should have kept her mouth shut.

"Why do you want to know?"

His question surprised her, but at least he hadn't shut their conversation down. "I'm just curious about your hopes and dreams, that's all. You appear out of nowhere, a soldier"—scarred in more ways than one—"and I want to know you better, Romeo. Is that a crime?"

The fallen trunk of a giant lay at the edge of the trail, its root system a big yawning cave. Camille was of a mind to climb up and explore. She stopped at the trail near the tree and pressed her hands against the trunk, looking for a place to climb up.

Romeo stopped walking and strolled to her side. "No, it's no crime." His dark mood had vanished. "But why don't you start first?"

"I. . .uh. . ." Camille found several roots that gave her traction and climbed onto the fallen trunk—at least ten feet in width, about half the size of some of the larger trees at the base.

"What are you doing?"

She giggled. "I've always wanted to do this."

"And you were afraid to ride my motorcycle?"

"Come on, this isn't nearly as dangerous. Unless I fell and no one knew where to find me."

"I get it. I'm here to see and hear you, in case you fall."

"Sort of like that question—if a tree falls in the forest and there's no one to hear it, did it really fall?"

"Right, but don't expect me to catch you. Are we clear?"

Camille stood up, spread her arms out for balance, and began walking across the fibrous, wrinkled bark. She laughed at the thrill of it. "Why, because that would be too cliché?"

"It would only be cliché if there were romance between us."

She wasn't sure she liked his words. What did he mean? Didn't he feel something between them? "And if there were romance between us, I would definitely expect you to catch me if I fell." *Try that on for a trick question, buddy.*

"You're changing the subject again. You're supposed to go first, remember? What are your hopes and dreams, Camille?"

Something in his voice drew her up short—he *really* wanted to know—and she found it difficult to focus on his question while balancing on a massive log. "For the longest time, I've dreamed of seeing the world—of escaping this little town, even though I love it. I want to win the art competition so I can get the scholarship and get my degree. Be successful. Then I can leave. . . ."

Spoken aloud, the words almost strangled her. They sounded too much like Alexa's dream.

"You might want to think through that decision carefully. I made a similar one when I enlisted. I didn't count the cost."

Thick emotions constricted her throat, making her cough.

She thrust her arms out again to gain her balance, but. . . She toppled, falling into oblivion. . . .

She screamed. Greens and browns streaked across her vision. This was going to hurt.

Lord, help me!

Sturdy arms seized her, breaking her fall, and pulled her close against a strong chest. Breathless, she clutched Romeo's shoulders.

"I've got you." He held her in his arms.

Heart pounding, Camille caught her breath. "Thank you." And she'd made those ridiculous comments about romance and clichés. "I really didn't expect that to happen."

Still holding her, he grinned. "I did."

"But. . ." He really didn't believe there was something between them?

While Camille searched his eyes, wanting the answer to that question and so many more, his gaze traveled over her face, down her neck, then back to her lips. So near him now, she didn't dare look away from his eyes.

There was something about Romeo, something inside him, that told her he was a man worth knowing. She could sense an inner strength in him. Nothing was more important to Camille. She allowed her gaze to drift to the misshapen skin on his face. She gently lifted her hand to touch his scar and hesitated.

"Romeo. . . I. . ." She pressed her hand against the left side of his face, wanting him to know how much she cared. . . .

Romeo tensed and squeezed her wrist. He pried her hand from the scar, stepped back, and released her to stand on her own, his expression dark.

❧

Camille stared up at him, eyes wide with hurt. Why was she looking at him like that? She didn't know anything about being hurt. Her lips parted like she wanted to say something, but no words came.

He looked away from her and to the trail. "I should get back," he said. He turned away from her and started walking, confusion and pain almost blinding his path.

"Wait." Camille grabbed his arm then let go.

Romeo stared at the ground, waiting. He knew she wanted him to look at her, but he couldn't.

"Romeo, I'm sorry." Her words were breathless. "I shouldn't have done that."

This time, he was the one who had no words. He shook his head then muttered, "You did nothing wrong."

And she hadn't. Not really. But she'd crossed an invisible line.

He left her standing there, wondering if she would follow. Shoving through the giant ferns, he eventually found the trail, the packed earth smoothed by the steps of thousands of visitors. He started toward the direction they'd walked, heading back. To what? To whom?

Mama was only trying to keep him busy, make him feel needed so he wouldn't leave her again. He could put Kent off for only so long. But he'd only considered Kent's job offer out of desperation, out of a lack of purpose.

Somehow, he had to get his life back.

But no, that wasn't right— What he needed was to forge a new life.

Romeo hesitated, listening. He couldn't hear Camille's footsteps behind him. Maybe he should wait for her. He shook his head and started walking again. No, she spent enough time alone in the forest. No need to worry about her.

He stopped again, remembering her expression when he'd found her—almost like she'd been afraid of something.

Or someone.

And he hadn't done what he'd come out here for in the first place—to discuss his idea about starting a business in town. Camille knew the business owners around here and should be able to offer advice or recommend him to someone who could.

Sighing, he broke into a run, wishing things had turned out differently. But it wasn't just the business stuff. With Camille, Romeo could forget about his appearance, forget about the past. Or at least he could until she touched his face.

He'd been mistaken. She was no different from anyone else who gaped at him. She couldn't get past the scar and measure him as a man, as a person. He wouldn't be whole ever again. Not with himself. Not with a woman.

How could he have been so wrong?

Up ahead he caught a glimpse of the parking lot, but he wasn't ready to leave. Not yet. Not till he calmed down. Romeo spotted a fallen tree a little ways from the trail. Ignoring the rules like Camille, he crunched through the ferns and needles, careful to leave the foliage unharmed. When he made it to the broken trunk, he sat on part of it.

Romeo hung his head. The pain inside was almost palpable. He shook at the memory of Camille's touch, and his shoulders shook as he cried without tears.

Lord, give me hope. Give me a future. . . .

nine

The next morning Camille almost stumbled down the stairs as she made her way to the kitchen. The aroma of freshly brewed coffee stirred her senses.

Last night, she'd been unable to sleep again. After what she'd done in the redwood forest, Romeo hadn't come to dinner. Neither had she continued reading Shakespeare or written a blog post—but she wasn't entirely sure that Romeo was to blame for that.

You have to eat breakfast, Romeo.

Camille was confident that his "mama" wouldn't let him skip it.

So, she'd wait for him. She had no idea what she would say once she saw him, but somehow she had to tell him how sorry she was. The last thing she'd ever want to do was hurt the man. And yet, why had she felt compelled to touch his face? Why had she believed she had a right?

The only good thing? She'd been able to convey all the torment she felt into the painting yesterday afternoon and had made substantial progress. Now all that remained was in the details. Those she could do over the next few days if she didn't get distracted.

Aunt Erin and Stella were conversing quietly when Camille stepped into the kitchen. They both looked up abruptly and stared. Camille ignored them and strolled by the table, needing that first mug of caffeine. She reached into the cabinet and grabbed her usual cup.

"I thought I'd join you for breakfast this morning," Camille said as she poured some coffee.

"Oh? What would you like? I can warm you a croissant, or..."

Camille turned and smiled warmly at her aunt. She kissed her on the cheek. "You're too good to me. I'll have what's left of breakfast." But maybe Romeo had already eaten.

With a slight frown, she tugged a chair from the table and sat, wrapping both hands around the warm mug. She glanced at Stella, who hadn't said a word.

Camille snatched up the last piece of bacon. "Don't worry. I'll make some more when Romeo comes down."

Stella gave a light shake of her head. "Romeo has already gone for the day."

Gone? Camille stopped chewing. She harbored the sense that one day he would ride off on his motorcycle and never return. Was today that day? Was Camille the reason?

"Before breakfast?" Camille wasn't convinced.

"A breakfast meeting. Romeo is trying to start a business in town." Stella picked up the newspaper, opening it with a *pop* and dismissing Camille.

Aunt Erin began cleaning up the dishes.

A new business? Why hadn't he mentioned it yesterday? Regret washed over her—she knew exactly why. Because she'd gotten too close. He'd probably come looking for her to discuss the business prospects with her. Camille's mood lifted. Romeo was considering staying in town.

The thought brought a measure of relief. She relaxed in the chair, wanting to find out more. "That's great news. That means—"

"Yes, that means he'll be staying." Stella whipped the paper away from her face. "He went to the park to find you yesterday to ask you about the local businesses, but when he returned. . ." Stella's chin quivered, and she blinked back tears. "What did you say to him, Camille?"

Camille froze. "I. . .why. . .nothing. I said nothing." And it was true.

"Don't lie to me. I can read my boy. You did or said something, and I want to know what it was."

Heat shot through Camille's body. She pushed back from the table and stood, trembling. The woman had no right to accuse her.

Aunt Erin squeezed her shoulder. "Now Stella, I know you love your boy, but you can't blame Camille for his moodiness, can you? You have to admit he has issues, and why shouldn't he? The poor man has seen things, endured things, the rest of us never will."

Camille exhaled, her anger gone. She couldn't stand to be the cause of ill will between the two old friends. She pressed her hand over Aunt Erin's. "It's all right, Aunt Erin. I think. . . I think, yes, I might have done something that hurt Romeo. I'm so sorry, Stella. I never meant to. . ."

Stella glared at Camille like a mama bear protecting her cub. But Romeo was a man. When would Stella realize that?

The woman stood and looked her in the eye. "I know his mood had everything to do with you. Now you listen to me." Stella pointed her finger in Camille's face.

Camille took a step back.

"Stella!" Aunt Erin's voice shook. "Stella"—this time, more controlled—"remember your place in my home. Camille said she was sorry."

Camille folded her arms and looked away, willing her heart rate to slow down.

Stella took a few deep breaths then slumped back into a chair. "I'm sorry. It's just the Italian mother in me. Before he died, my husband used to tell me that I couldn't control my emotions, my outrage. The Meretes have always been impulsive"—she threw her hands up—"they act before they think. That's exactly what Romeo did the day he enlisted— he was reacting to his father. You'd think I had Merete blood running in my veins, too. I told Romeo's father that I had lived with him too long."

A distant look came into Stella's eyes, and Camille wondered if she was thinking about her late husband. Camille wanted to say something, anything, to bring happiness back into Stella's eyes.

But before she could speak, Stella continued, "You can't blame a mother for watching out for her boy, can you?"

Camille sighed and slipped back into her chair, wanting to dial down the tension in the room. And if Stella had been willing, then how could Camille do otherwise? "No, I can't blame you, Stella. And I'm very sorry. I couldn't have known. . . ." Camille toyed with her napkin, hoping she could avoid telling Stella that she'd touched Romeo's scar. That he'd had a strong reaction, perhaps even a "Merete" reaction. Camille sucked in a breath.

"Romeo was promised to a beautiful girl once," Stella said. "*Tesoro*. . . She was such a treasure."

Camille winced. Did she mean that Camille wasn't beautiful enough for Romeo, nor was she anything to be treasured? She glanced at Aunt Erin, but the woman had once again busied herself cleaning the breakfast dishes.

"Then one night he and his father argued, and Romeo left. He enlisted. Can you believe it? Throwing everything away—the business, his family, and even his girl. Eventually, he did ask Maria to marry him. They were to be married the week he arrived home from Afghanistan."

Stella's words stung Camille. Romeo said he had once been in love. Could he still love this woman? Her throat ached, but she forced the question. "What happened?"

"Romeo was injured in an explosion." Stella gave her head a fierce shake. "Everything changed."

No wonder Romeo was so hurt—his fiancée must have broken off the engagement. *Oh Romeo. . .*

"You must be asking yourself why I am telling you this. Because Camille, you are making plans to leave us, and I cannot stand by and watch my Romeo get hurt again." Stella bolted from the kitchen and left Camille and Aunt Erin in stunned silence.

Aunt Erin sat next to Camille and patted her hand. "Is

there something. . .serious between you and Romeo? What have I missed?"

Frowning, Camille tore the paper napkin to shreds. "Nothing. No. . . There's nothing between us."

"Are you sure about that?"

"It's not like I'm dating the man. He hasn't been here that long. No, there's no reason for Stella to be worried." Even if there were something between them, Camille could hardly believe the woman's reaction. Still, she understood—a little. The man had been devastated in ways that Camille could never understand.

"Perhaps the feelings are on Romeo's side then, and not yours."

What could Camille say? That Romeo thrilled her to the core? That yes, she longed for Romeo to kiss her, to hold her in his arms? She wanted to know him, everything about him. But after what Stella shared today. . . Camille sighed. "I don't know how Romeo feels, but Stella is right, of course. I'm hoping to win the contest. And if I do, I'll leave town."

"Yes, I know it's your dream to get an art degree. But on the off chance that you don't win, what will you do? Will you find a way to go anyway? Just like your sister?"

Just like your sister." The words burned through her. "If I don't finish my painting, there's no chance I'm going to win." Camille stood. "I'll see you later."

Camille dressed and left for the UPS store to ship a few of her bags off to a new client. Her small business was growing—if only slightly—but this wasn't really her dream. Her bags meant income to pay rent and survive. And today, they were keeping her from the portrait. A portrait she shouldn't have painted without permission, given the way Romeo responded to her touch yesterday. And yes, his reaction had fueled her inspiration. Still, how could she enter it in the contest without discussing it with him?

And winning would mean leaving him.

Oh Romeo. *Why, Lord? Why did You send this man into my life? To confuse me? To throw me off?*

She'd had a plan for the future until Romeo came into her life. But he wasn't really in her life—he was simply in the house where she now lived. If she could avoid running into him, could she stay on track?

On the drive home, she worked to shove aside her anxiety over Stella's words and Romeo's reaction to her touch—she needed to just paint when she got home. She turned down the street and then into the driveway.

In the shadows on the side of the house, someone dangled from the window before jumping.

આ

Italian music piped through the speaker above Romeo's head as he sat at the booth at Bernardino's restaurant. He'd left the house earlier this morning, claiming he had a breakfast appointment. And he did, with himself—he wanted to be out of the house before he had to face Camille. He needed time to think. He rode his bike around the little town, assessing various locations.

He'd ended up at Bernardino's. The clock on the wall said ten thirty. Call it an early lunch or late breakfast, or better, brunch—Romeo wanted to get a feel for the clientele. The waitress had taken his order of his favorites, bruschetta and a cappucino, without looking at him. Not once.

Romeo sighed. Kent had called this morning, pestering him about the job offer. He'd served with Kent, whose family also owned a business—the motorcycle shop in Tucson where Romeo had purchased his bike. But, unlike Romeo's mother, Kent's family maintained the business, and Kent had a job waiting for him once his tour of duty was complete.

Romeo had planned to face his mother and assure himself that she was in a good place, then move on. But she'd planted a seed in him, like she always did. The quaint little Victorian village was beginning to grow on him, and a vision was beginning to grow *in* him. After Camille had touched his face, doing what no other person dared, Romeo thought he would crumble like a building that had been bombed too many times.

He'd had nowhere else to turn but God—and wasn't that His way? All Romeo had needed was to spend time with Him, and then peace would calm his troubled thoughts.

And then, with the slight lifting of the rubble from his heart, Romeo drove through town. And drove past a FOR SALE sign in the corner of the window of Bernardino's.

Could this be God's will for his future? Here in Redbrook he could be a good son and make up for going AWOL on his mother. Here, he could build a future. He took a sip of his cappuccino.

Here, he would have to forget about Camille. She'd torn away the scab over his heart, exposing a lot of buried emotions. Longing, elation, hope—then humiliation, dread, and pain. He could actually feel an ache in his gut when she'd touched his disfigured face.

Romeo squeezed his eyes shut.

"Sir, your order," the waitress said.

Romeo opened his eyes. She set his plate on the table. His mouth watered at the bruschetta—grilled bread with various toppings. He'd asked for extra virgin olive oil and prosciutto, thinly sliced cured ham. Perfect.

The waitress smiled and left, again without looking at him. If Romeo bought the place, some staffing changes were definitely in order.

As he ate in silence, sitting in a dark corner, he observed the customers. Lots of tourists came in, toting cameras and maps. Some of the customers had a sort of artsy flair—probably locals. Romeo considered what he might do to add a little Merete zest to the place. An olive bar, perhaps?

He finished the last bite of bread and thought back to the night he'd argued with his father. The family business was meant for his sons, Dad said. But what if Romeo had different plans? He didn't, but did anyone ask him? Nope.

His parents were grooming Emilio to take over anyway. Romeo had counted on his big brother running the restaurant.

But then Emilio died, leaving Romeo to take his place. A year later, everything fell apart.

Romeo always dreamed of seeing the world, or at least having some options in life. Somehow the conversation with Dad escalated to an argument. Romeo tore off his apron and stalked from the kitchen, fuming that his life had already been chosen for him.

He skipped work the next day and trudged the streets of Greenwood, Indiana. He found himself standing in front of a US Army recruiting office.

The irony of it—he joined the military to get away. Then his father died and Mama sold the business while he was gone, leaving him nothing to come back to. Now he was trying to rebuild what he'd lost—a restaurant. He'd come full circle.

He hung his head over the plate.

The decision to enlist had been a rash one, born of bitterness. His impulsive behavior had cost him everything.

He'd returned a broken man.

"The Lord is near to the brokenhearted and saves those who are crushed in spirit."

The simple scripture, read to him by a chaplain who visited him daily in the military hospital, suddenly came to mind. He'd tried to run from the pain, to grow calloused in the face of it, but Camille's touch had broken open the wounds of his heart.

God was the only one who could save him now.

When he raised his head, he found himself staring into the mirror on the other side of the room.

Romeo's reflection mocked him.

ten

Romeo jumped on his Suzuki and zoomed away from the restaurant. He wanted to speak with the owner, but the man wasn't there, so Romeo would need to make an appointment. Was this another rash decision? How could he afford to buy the place?

Getting the details couldn't hurt, however. He took his time driving through downtown and various shopping centers—sort of a restaurant row—and wished he had talked to Camille about his idea yesterday. He needed her perspective, but he'd been avoiding her. He wondered if he could face her again anytime soon.

But he had to do it, since he was staying in the same house.

Where Camille was concerned, Romeo was beyond torn. The woman forced him to look inside himself, to push past his self-loathing, his insecurities.

As he turned down the street to her house, he wished he could make a silent approach. His bike wasn't exactly a quiet ride.

A police cruiser was parked at the curb in front of the house.

What... A lump rose in Romeo's throat.

He gunned the bike and turned into the driveway. An officer was sitting in the cruiser. Romeo jumped from his bike, tugged off his helmet, and ran to the house.

He burst through the door. "Mama!"

"In here." Her voice came from the kitchen.

Romeo bolted through the doorway. Erin and Mama sat at the kitchen table. Both women looked worn and pale. Erin's hand shook as she poured coffee.

"What happened? Why is a police officer out front?"

Mama pressed her hands against the table to stand.

"No, don't get up." Romeo set his helmet on a chair and tugged off his jacket, concern growing by the second. "Just tell me."

"We had an intruder today," Erin said.

His heart missed a beat. "An intruder? What do you mean?"

"Someone broke into the house."

"Someone robbed you? In the middle of the day?" A surge of energy shot through Romeo. He paced, shoving his hand through his hair. "Was anyone hurt?"

His pulse raced. Where was Camille?

"Calm yourself," Mama said. "No one was hurt."

He collapsed into a chair. "Can someone please tell me what happened?"

Both women seemed to be stuck in a state of disbelief.

"Camille came home and saw someone jumping from a window," Erin said.

"Where is she?" But he already knew.

He bounded up the stairs, forgetting his decision to avoid her.

At the door, he paused. The last time he'd intruded in her space, she wasn't happy. He could hear her sniffles on the other side of the door. Everything inside Romeo screamed for him to go to her, to comfort her, to keep her safe. And despite his many doubts, he knew she was worth the risk. Without knocking, he gently pushed the door open.

Camille stood in the middle of the room staring at the canvas on her easel, which faced away from Romeo, tears sliding down her cheeks. She looked up at him, and her eyes flashed wide.

"What"—she wiped her cheeks with the backs of her hands—"what are you doing here?"

Romeo took one more step into the room then hesitated.

"I heard that someone broke into the house. I wanted to see if you were all right."

She sniffed again, glanced at the canvas, then whipped a cloth over it. "I'm not hurt, if that's what you're asking."

"So you saw this person? What was he after? Did he steal any valuables?"

"In a manner of speaking, yes, he stole something from me. Time. A chance at winning the art contest."

Confused, Romeo frowned. But overpowered by his desire to comfort her, he ignored her wary tone and moved to stand next to her.

"He destroyed my painting."

"What?" Romeo didn't know what to say. "Oh Camille, I'm so sorry." He reached for her.

That was all the invitation she needed. With one step she was in his arms. He wrapped them around her, and she sobbed into his shoulder. In all his imaginings of holding her, he'd never wanted it to be like this, because of this.

But now that she was here. . .

Romeo savored the smell of her hair, the feel of her slight form against his. All his wrangling over avoiding Camille slipped through his fingers like the past.

&

A calm settled over Camille, now that she'd soaked Romeo's shirt with her tears.

She drew in a deep breath, filling her head with the scent of him. She could stay enveloped in the cocoon that was Romeo forever. If she stayed long enough, would she morph into something beautiful? The ridiculous thought had come out of nowhere. She must be getting tired.

When she sensed it was time to leave the shelter of his arms, she took a step back. Again, she wiped her eyes, her cheeks, and her face. "I'm so sorry about sobbing in your shirt. I'm totally embarrassed."

"Don't be." His eyes were gentle.

Camille moved away from the canvas, over to her desk. She wasn't prepared for Romeo to see what was hidden under the cloth. "I was shocked, that's all."

That and Stella's tale had worn on Camille. She was going away, or at least doing everything in her power to leave. She couldn't allow herself to care about Romeo or allow him to care about her. Yet, only hours after hearing Stella's lament, Camille found herself in his arms. She glanced at Romeo, still standing next to the covered painting. She looked in his eyes.

The depth of concern she saw there flooded her with an emotion she couldn't name. A thick knot expanded in her throat—she'd never needed someone else to be strong for her.

But Romeo seemed to be changing all of that.

Camille tugged her attention away and moved the mouse to wake the computer from sleep mode.

"Why would someone want to destroy your painting?"

Camille brought up her blog to see if there were any new comments. She had to draw Romeo away from the canvas.

In reply, she shook her head, thinking. "There are only a few days left before I have to deliver the painting to the contest. It will be on display during the art fair."

"Someone destroyed it because they were jealous? Didn't want you to win? Is that it?"

There. She pulled up the blog on the computer. She could distract him with that, she hoped. Staring at the computer screen, she tugged the roller chair from the desk and sat. "Have you seen my blog, *In Love with Shakespeare*?"

Romeo moved her direction. When he stood beside her, she glanced up and smiled. "I read a scene from one of Shakespeare's plays every night, or as often as I can, then I write blog posts about it, though I'm off my schedule this week."

Since you arrived.

Romeo leaned down to read the computer screen, his face

close to hers. "I meant to ask you about this when I heard your friend at that store mention it. You have a lot of things going on. Why the interest in Shakespeare?"

The question sparked an idea in Camille. Excited, she sat tall. "Why the interest in Shakespeare? Have you ever read Shakespeare?"

He looked mystified.

Camille burst out laughing, and Romeo grinned. She thought he wanted to laugh but held it back for some reason.

"What's so funny?" he asked.

"You're named after one of Shakespeare's most famous characters, so the question sounded a little ironic coming from you, that's all."

"You'll have to talk to my mother about why she named me Romeo, but I am absolutely positive it had nothing to do with Shakespeare. It's a common Italian name, Camille."

"I have an idea. Would you. . . No, forget it."

"What? Don't do that to me. Say it."

"Well, if you insist." Camille stared at her computer screen and gave him a cursory, teasing glance. "Would you be interested in reading Shakespeare with me? I could read it to you in the evenings. Sort of like a discussion group of two. That's partly why I started the blog, so I could discuss my thoughts with others."

The disturbing comment was still there on the screen, but she ignored it. She would not let it overshadow this moment. She was about to embark on reading Shakespeare with Romeo. Now, there was a blog post!

"Thanks for asking. I'd like that."

"Really?" She hadn't seriously believed he would agree. But maybe he wanted to spend time with her. The idea warmed her heart a little. She needed something to take her mind off the fact that someone had invaded her attic and destroyed her painting.

My painting. Her spirits sank a little again. Romeo had

been far too sensitive yesterday when she touched his scar. She could hardly show him the painting now. Not until she'd had a chance to explain first.

She skimmed the comments section to see if there were more strange messages from Don John. Nothing. She exhaled and sat back, smiling. "So let's start tonight."

"Right after you show me the painting."

Camille glanced up and saw Romeo lifting the cloth. "No!"

eleven

Romeo sat in the backyard with Mama, listening to her talk about her plans for painting the house. He wished he could get a word in edgewise to remind her that this was Erin's house, not hers. For all he knew, Erin was happy to have a take-charge person running her life.

He stared at the petunias, watching Mama dig while she chattered away. He was surprised she hadn't persuaded him to work on the garden, too, but she enjoyed this herself, despite her arthritis. Planting flowers was therapeutic.

Though he tried to pay attention to her discussion of possible house colors, he kept thinking about Camille and her refusal to show him the painting. Why the big deal? Her secretiveness piqued his curiosity. To think that someone had broken in and destroyed it. . . .

Tension snaked through Romeo's shoulders, and he leaned forward in the chair. He'd like to get his hands on the jerk. Surely Camille had some clue about who did it and why. But she insisted there were too many people within the artistic community who knew that she was entering the contest to single out one person.

He didn't believe that for a minute. She was hiding more than her painting.

Mama was staring at him. "Have you heard a word I've said?"

"I. . .uh. . . Yes." He'd heard her talking, no doubt there.

"Stella," Erin said, calling from the deck. "Margaret is here. She stopped by, so I've invited her to stay for tea. You, too, Romeo, if you'd care to listen to us old ladies nattering."

Mama looked displeased at first, then her face lit up. "I'll be back, my little darlings," she said to the flowers, then began her feeble attempt to rise.

"Let me help you." Romeo gripped her hand gently and cupped her elbow to steady her, assisting her to her feet.

"Oh dear. My knees are dirty."

Romeo laughed. "So change your clothes. Your friend can wait."

Living here was good for Mama. To her credit, she hadn't asked him one word about her idea for opening an Italian restaurant here in town. Difficult as it had to be, she was being patient, which showed him just how much she wanted him to stay.

As he watched her make her way to the deck, he spotted Camille lingering at the corner of the house, just out of Mama's sight. He might have laughed if he wasn't so conflicted where Camille was concerned. Before he'd met her, he'd only *thought* he had issues.

Once Mama was inside, Camille meandered from the side of the house, her hands behind her back, as if she'd just come to peruse the garden.

"Oh." She gasped. "I didn't realize you were here."

Her teasing smile gave her away.

Attempting to ignore the way she made his heart race, Romeo sighed and relaxed against the chair. Mama's unplanted petunias looked limp and pathetic next to the garden gnome. They needed nourishment.

And he needed to get a life.

Starting a business in this little Victorian-style town sounded good on the surface. But could he stand to be near a woman who complicated his life, even when she wasn't trying?

Her simple touch somehow led to the deep places in his heart. Yet she wasn't willing to open herself up to him and show him the painting.

Camille dropped to her knees and picked up where Mama left off.

"You think you're helping, but Mama likes the therapy. She's not going to be happy if you finish planting the flowers."

Camille stopped digging and looked at Romeo, squinting at the sun behind him. "I hadn't thought of that."

She scrambled to her feet and stood to look at him. Her colorful, tie-dyed T-shirt was a little large for her. It fluttered in the breeze, reminding him of the very first time he'd seen her—except for the dirt stuck to her knees. Camille blended into the artsy, natural culture of the town, and right now, she reminded him of...an earth girl.

Earth Girl plopped into the lawn chair next to him, her flowery scent wrapping around him. "I came to apologize."

Romeo pressed his lips into a smile and glanced at her, waiting.

"Things haven't been the same between us since, well, since I..." She sighed. "Since in the forest when I—"

"It's okay. You don't have to say it. Apology accepted."

Camille turned to face him. "I have to say it. Saying it will get everything out in the open."

"What if I don't want to get everything out in the open? Don't I get a choice?"

"Romeo, you need to heal."

Romeo worked to keep his rising ire in check. Who was she to talk to him like this? She'd already pushed him too far.

"The only way to heal an open, seeping wound is to let the air caress it, the sun shine on it."

Romeo fought the need to get up and walk away. But that would be a repeat of yesterday. Why wasn't he strong enough to listen?

"Why aren't you saying anything?" she asked.

"I accepted your apology, so can we move on now?"

"There is nothing I would like more than to move on. And in order to do that we have to talk about what happened. I touched the scar on your face, well, because I"—her breathing grew fast and deep, mirroring his own—"I care deeply about you. And well, you see, I'm an artist. It's the way I connect. I need to touch and feel and understand before I. . ."

Romeo laughed, surprising himself, but he knew it was the quickest way to shield himself from the pain she was stirring up inside. Still, the defense mechanism wouldn't hold up long.

A tabby cat zipped across the backyard, right over the petunias. Not far behind, a large brown-and-white mutt raced by them, barking and chasing the poor feline. The dog trampled the flowers.

Camille yelped. She stood so fast, the lawn chair toppled behind her. Then a red-haired boy of about ten ran past.

"Hi, Camille! Can you help? I've got to get Flanders before he kills Mrs. Haskin's cat."

"And before he reaches Mr. Dunnigan's yard!" Camille shouted after him. With wide eyes, she glanced at Romeo then took off after the boy, yelling, "The town hermit will torture you in his dungeon."

Romeo stared after her.

"You going to help Jared or what?" she yelled over her shoulder.

Grinning, he jogged after her and slipped between the boards of the broken privacy fence. Mama hadn't seen this, or she would have set him to hammering already. Stepping into the neighbor's backyard, he realized Camille and gang had already crossed into the next. As he jogged between a swing set and a fishpond filled with koi, a woman stepped out the back door, her face slathered in cold cream, a cucumber slice covering one eye.

Romeo waved and kept going. "Trying to catch a dog— sorry!"

He caught up to Camille, standing next to one of the widest pines he'd ever seen. She leaned over, catching her breath. Flanders barked up the tree while the boy tried to figure out how to climb it.

"Is that your cat?" Romeo asked.

"Nope," Jared said.

"Then why not just leave it and take the dog? It'll come down sooner or later."

Camille gasped. "Are you crazy? This is Dunnigan's yard. Miriam will never be seen again if we don't return her to Mrs. Haskin. And Jared will be blamed."

Romeo frowned. "You can't be serious."

Camille crossed her eyes then smiled at Romeo. "Kids always have their little myths and legends about the local hermit. Mr. Dunnigan is it."

"Huh," Romeo said. It was all he could manage.

"We have to be gone before Mr. Dunnigan notices we're here or be prepared to battle him. I didn't bring my sword, did you?" Camille asked.

Her teasing smile did crazy things to his head.

"He sounds like an interesting character."

Jared had already climbed onto the first limb.

Could Romeo really stand by and watch him do it? What if he got hurt? "Wait, I'll do it."

"No, I got this," Jared called down.

The cat was high. "Uh, I don't feel comfortable with this. You could get hurt."

❧

Camille could hardly believe what she was seeing. Romeo was halfway up the old pine—Miriam kept climbing higher to get away from him. Maybe this wasn't such a good idea.

Jared kept looking back at Mr. Dunnigan's house, dread written on his face.

"Don't worry," Camille said. "I'm here with you. Romeo is here. You're going to be fine. He'll get the cat."

Jared hung his head. "Mom said if the dog got out again, we'd have to take him to the pound."

"Oh no, she can't mean that." Camille hoped his mom's

words were just an idle threat.

A limb cracked above, jerking her attention back to the tree. Romeo had the cat—thank goodness—and was slowly making his way back down. But Jared's dog was still barking.

"Jared, why don't you take Flanders home? We'll make sure Miriam is returned."

"I guess you're right. Thanks for your help. Before I go, can I ask you about your friend? What happened to his face?"

Deep sadness filled Camille—this was what Romeo had to go through every day of his life. She ran her hand over Jared's head. "He was injured in Afghanistan. He's a hero."

"Wow. . . ." Jared drug the word out with awe then grabbed Flanders by the collar and scolded him as he tugged him from the yard.

Soon Romeo reached the bottom limb. "You ready?" He held the cat down to her.

Camille raised her arms. "Sure, let her drop."

He released the terrified feline inches from Camille. She caught her and immediately began to speak in soothing tones, rubbing the poor thing behind the ears. The cat began to purr loudly.

Romeo dropped to the ground, landing on his feet. He let out a breath.

"Thank you." She looked in his eyes. There she saw raw pain. "You heard?"

He swallowed. "You'd think I'd be used to that by now."

"What's going on out here?" Mr. Dunnigan stood on his deck, as cantankerous as ever.

Camille tugged Romeo's wrist and dragged him through the gate in the privacy fence.

"What are you doing?" he asked. "Why didn't you answer Mr. Dunnigan?"

Camille kept going, Romeo on her heels, jogging behind her.

"Mr. Dunnigan eats it up. He'd never admit it, but he loves

that the kids think he's a crazy hermit. Keeping up the act keeps kids out of his yard for the most part."

"Are you crazy?" he asked.

"Oh, don't worry. I take him cookies all the time. It's all in good fun."

Instead of going through the neighbors' yards to make their way home, Camille had a better idea. "Follow me."

She led him through the wooded area that bordered the neighborhood backyards. Large pine, maple, and oak trees populated the area, along with ferns and thick foliage. A few younger redwoods remained, but most had been lumbered from the area years ago.

"Where are we going?" Romeo stepped behind her as she made her way through the undergrowth.

"I'm going to let Miriam go in the woods behind Mrs. Haskin's house. That's where she normally hangs out."

Miriam finished rubbing against Camille's legs and ran away when she heard Mrs. Haskin's call. Camille risked a glance at Romeo and found him smiling at her, the pain in his eyes lessened.

They were in the woods again. Yesterday came flooding back. She wanted to reach up and touch his face again and make him let her help him.

Before she knew it, he was squeezing her wrist. She'd reached for him without even realizing it.

He sucked in a breath. "Camille, please don't."

"But. . . But why? Right now, it's the only thing standing between us."

"It's not the only thing, but that's beside the point. Why is the scar on my face so important to you?"

"Because it's important to you. You have allowed it to define you."

Romeo released a heavy sigh and hung his head. Then he lifted his face, looking to the treetops. "All the trees are tall here—even the ones that aren't redwoods."

"Yes." Camille studied him, trying to read him.

"We should head back to the house, don't you think?" he asked.

Disappointment seeped in. He wasn't going to open up. At that moment, Camille wasn't exactly sure why she was so determined to make him. As he made his way between the trees, she was the one to follow this time, which gave her a chance to admire Romeo's broad shoulders and lean physique.

In the woods behind Aunt Erin's house, he stopped and turned to face Camille. "All right, I'll tell you what you want to know, but you have to show me your painting."

Camille's throat tightened. Romeo didn't know that the scar on his face and her painting were linked. She wasn't sure she had a specific question for him, but she'd give it a shot. "Okay, why did it bother you so much when I touched your face?"

"I'm sure you can guess. There's a lot of the past tied up in what happened to me. I have a hideous scar to remind me of my mistakes every day." Romeo found a fallen tree trunk and sat.

Camille sat next to him, appreciating the fact he was opening up, and how difficult it must be. A few seconds passed. She waited in silence, not wanting to press him. A chipmunk flitted onto a rock and stared at them then scurried around looking for food.

"Mama always told me I was so handsome that I could have any woman I wanted. She called me her handsome Romeo. But I didn't want just any woman. I wanted Maria. And now—look at me." His tone was strained.

Camille wished she hadn't pushed him. Clearly he wasn't ready.

He took a deep breath. "You asked if I had ever been in love. I told you yes. But that's not all. I loved her very much. But I enlisted without even thinking about what that would do to her, to our future together. I left her behind. I left Mama and the family business behind.

"Don't get me wrong." He sat a little straighter. "I'm proud to have served. It was an honor. And Maria was faithful to write letters. We made plans to get married during my next leave." He paused, his shoulders slumping. "Then a roadside bomb exploded. Three members of our group were killed." He swallowed. "Two of us survived. Injured."

"I'm so sorry." Camille's words came out in a whisper as she imagined the horrors of war. "You don't have to go on. I'm so sorry for forcing you to remember this."

He shook his head. "You've brought us both to this place, and now we have to go forward. I lost a good part of my face that day. I had a lot of reconstructive surgeries, and. . . I couldn't take any more."

Camille swallowed. "Your mother told me some of the story, and I know that your fiancée left you. You don't need to relive this because of my stupidity."

"No, Camille." He shook his head. "That's not what happened. Maria was faithful. She didn't leave me. I'm the one who broke off the engagement. War. . . It somehow changed me. No matter what I looked like on the outside, with or without this hideous scar, I was a different person on the inside."

"I don't understand."

"I loved Maria too much to allow her to marry a complete stranger. To make her pay for my mistakes." Romeo chuckled and shook his head. "I didn't think I could ever talk about this."

How could she ever understand what he'd been through? She'd lived a sheltered life in comparison.

He raised his eyebrows at her. "And now, I want to see your painting." He pushed himself from the log and began walking toward the house.

"Wait." Camille grabbed his arm. This time she held on.

"Let me explain it first." Dread suffused her. She'd made a mistake, but there was no going back.

Romeo frowned. "You've really got me puzzled."

Camille felt desperate. She had to make him understand. "I had been praying for inspiration for a new painting that day—the day we met. The first time I saw you, I knew you had become my new inspiration. Romeo, I painted you."

His face morphed through a series of painful expressions before apprehension settled in his eyes.

She took a deep breath and exhaled. "I painted you without your scar."

twelve

Darkness had settled by the time Romeo made his way to Clearing, his motorcycle rumbling beneath him. The little town was about an hour north of Redbrook. An hour. He'd driven an hour. He would have kept going, too, except he needed to fill up his tank. He managed to catch every red light as he drove through the quaint town, looking for a gas station. Finally, on the far right corner, a Shell station beckoned.

Romeo pulled up to the pump and turned off the ignition. He tugged off his helmet and strolled inside to pay for the gas. Back at the pump as he filled the tank, he couldn't help but beat himself up. He'd done it again.

Maybe he was running from his problems. Or maybe going for a motorcycle ride was good therapy. His mother enjoyed planting gardens and nurturing plants. Riding his bike did the same for Romeo.

Of all the things he'd expected to hear from Camille—all the possibilities of what she'd painted—he'd never expected to hear that she'd painted *him*.

And. . . She painted him without his scar. That told him everything about what she saw when she looked at him. He was hideous and broken, and she needed to fix him. Her painting was a testimony of that—and though it was only one painting, it might as well have been a million the way it crushed him.

Heaviness pressed his shoulders. He had no idea what to think or how to feel.

Just when he finally opened up to her, she pushed him further away. And now he was back in the abyss of self-loathing and shame and pain that he'd worked to avoid from the beginning.

Her words were like a salty ocean wave against a festering wound—only worse. Romeo had to get away.

So he left without seeing the painting. Without saying good-bye to Mama.

But he'd not had the words. A motorcycle gang riding Harleys waited at the red light across the way, gunning their engines. Romeo hoped they wouldn't stop at the gas station. He was in no mood to talk about his bike and his travels.

The light turned green, and they waved at Romeo as they passed. He waved back and spotted a small theater across the way. Clearing Shakespearean Playhouse.

He released a long breath and replaced the gas nozzle. No matter where he went, something reminded him of Camille.

On a sudden impulse Romeo drove across the street and parked in the crowded lot next to the theater. If he hurried, maybe he could catch whatever was playing. Maybe it would take his mind from his troubles. And maybe he could understand Camille's Shakespeare fixation.

Thinking about everything that had happened hadn't done one thing to solve his problems.

Hadn't Jesus said that worrying couldn't change a hair on a person's head? Romeo knew that firsthand. He stood in a short line at the box office to buy a ticket.

"Sorry, mate." The ticket taker behind the window shrugged. "I just sold the last two to the guy ahead of you."

Figures. Romeo sagged. "Mind if I look around inside?"

"No skin off my back." He winced at Romeo's face. "If you're gonna try to sneak in, they ask for tickets at the door."

"Thanks," Romeo said, then went into the theater.

The foyer looked like a small Renaissance fair with several actors dressed in character. A juggler danced as he tossed colorful balls, and a flutist played Old English music. The atmosphere was lively and expectant as patrons made their way into the auditorium to see *Romeo and Juliet.*

He'd never been able to understand Shakespearean English

in school and doubted he'd enjoy the play anyway. But he'd looked forward to listening to Camille read Shakespeare.

Romeo meandered to a back corner. A small lamp rested on a table, and a couple of candles flickered in sconces on either side of a soldier's photograph. The small gold-plated epigraph at the bottom of the frame read, IN MEMORY OF OUR SON, JAMES JOHNSON, A TRUE HERO.

Rubbing the good side of his face, Romeo stared at the young man wearing his navy uniform. Where had he served? What had killed him? The parents were probably still grieving. He survived the blast that had taken half his face, but others in his unit hadn't. And yet, Romeo had only now come to visit his mother. He hung his head, ashamed.

Unlike the man in this photograph, Romeo had come home.

"Can I help you?" A man's voice spoke from behind.

Romeo turned to find a man about his father's age, if he had been still alive. The man eyed Romeo's face, not unkindly, then met his gaze. "I saw you looking at that picture of my son. He died in Iraq."

"I'm sorry," Romeo said.

"But you were luckier, weren't you?"

Luckier? The man considered death a worse fate than Romeo's mutilated face. Of course. Words failed him. He hesitated then asked, "How did you know?"

"You have the look of a soldier about you, son. You're a hero. And you're welcome to watch any of the plays for free."

"Thank you," Romeo said, his chest tightening.

"This little corner is our tribute to our son. It's not much, but it's all we could do to honor him."

Suddenly the pressure eased, and Romeo began to understand. Camille was simply trying to pay him tribute. She'd painted him whole because she saw past the scar to the man, the hero. Warmth swelled inside. He should be honored by her portrait, not offended.

"Thanks." Romeo grabbed the man's hand and shook it as he backed out of the corner.

"Where are you going? Don't you want to see the play?"

From across the foyer, Romeo pressed his back against the glass door, shoving it open. "Not tonight. I've got something I need to take care of."

☙

Sweet Lorraine wasn't in class tonight. The woman lived for her art classes and wouldn't have missed one for anything. Camille frowned, allowing her concern for the elderly woman—eighty-seven and counting—to overshadow her misery over the pain she'd caused Romeo.

Oh, how she'd hurt him. She'd almost canceled class, but she couldn't afford to lose the money. Plus, her students were counting on her. Pushing her distress aside for the class had been difficult.

When she told Romeo about her portrait of him, the look on his face had nearly done her in. She'd followed him around the side of the house to his motorcycle, but he drove off without saying a word. Without looking at her.

A knot started in her throat. Camille drew in a breath. She had to focus right now. Tonight she was teaching the class how to deepen perspective and use cooler shades in the background to enhance the appearance of distance. Walking among the easels again, she was keenly aware of the empty place where Lorraine should be. Though everyone appeared focused on doing their best, hoping for praise from her, she could sense their discouragement. These were sensitive, artistic people.

Aunt Erin suggested that one of her students had destroyed her painting. They knew Camille had entered the contest, and they knew what winning would mean for them. They would lose their art teacher. Also, she was instructing several of them on their own paintings for entrance in the same contest.

As Camille studied each of her students, she couldn't bring herself to believe any one of them could be that cruel or violent. Breaking into someone's home to destroy something was a vicious act. And a crime.

She brushed the ridiculous idea aside. She had too much to think about tonight. She cleared her throat. "Listen up, everyone. I'm sorry that I'm somewhat distracted. But as you can see, Lorraine isn't here, and I'm worried about her. Would you mind if we finished up early tonight and then tacked on an extra fifteen minutes next week?"

Several nodded while others voiced their agreement, then everyone began cleaning up their workstations. Matt kept glancing toward Camille as she cleaned her own paintbrushes. When most of the class had left, he hovered, reluctant to leave. Camille wasn't in the mood for conversation, but apparently he wasn't willing to go away without one.

He cleared his throat.

She locked her desk then looked at Matt. "Did you need something?"

"I have a gift for you."

Not again. "A gift? Oh, Matt, you don't need. . ."

Matt lifted his painting of the brook in the redwoods and handed it to Camille.

She didn't have the heart to refuse. "It's beautiful, but you shouldn't have."

"I wanted to give it to you because you love it so much. You're the only one who appreciates my talents."

Her shoulders tensed. What could she say to that? Carrying the painting, she headed to the door. "Oh, Matt, I'm sure there are plenty of people who see how talented you are."

"Here, let me carry that for you." Matt took the painting from her and followed her out.

Camille allowed him to place the painting in her backseat, then she climbed into her car. Matt stood next to her door as she buckled her seat belt.

"Good night, Matt. See you next week."

Disappointment spilled from his eyes. Finally, he left her car and made his way to his little red sports car—a Mitsubishi Eclipse.

She hadn't thanked Matt enough. Still, what did he expect? A kiss?

Tonight wasn't the best of nights for gift giving. She should make it her policy not to accept gifts from her students.

She started her car and kept it in PARK while she called Lorraine on her cell. It was against the law to drive while talking on a mobile phone in California, and she hadn't upgraded to anything so fancy as Bluetooth or hands free. If she couldn't get an answer, she'd go over to the woman's house to check on her. She'd been there once or twice over the last year for lunch.

"Hello?" Lorraine answered.

Relieved, Camille started her car. "Lorraine! You weren't in class tonight. Is everything all right?"

"Oh goodness, yes. A good friend of mine had a stroke, and I spent most of the day at the hospital with her. I'm afraid I was too tired for class. I should have called."

"I'm sorry to hear about your friend, but I'm glad that you're okay."

"Thank you so much for checking on me. You're such a thoughtful young woman. I can't imagine why you aren't married yet."

Camille chuckled. Aunt Erin kept trying to convince Camille she didn't need a man, but Sweet Lorraine had a different opinion. "I suppose God hasn't sent me the right man yet."

"I'll be sure to talk to the Almighty about that in my prayers tonight."

"You do that. Good night, Lorraine. Take care."

On the drive home, thoughts of Romeo slammed Camille.

How could she ever make it up to him? She'd ruined everything. She couldn't help but think that even if God sent her someone, she would somehow end up destroying things.

Where Romeo was concerned, Stella had cautioned Camille to keep her distance because she was leaving. She agreed with Romeo's mother. Starting something between them and then leaving to fulfill her goals and dreams would be cruel.

And yet, she couldn't stay away from him. Lorraine was wrong—Camille wasn't a thoughtful young woman at all.

Camille pulled into the driveway and spotted Romeo's motorcycle. Her heart leaped with joy and relief, then dread weighed her down. Still, she had to know. She had to see him. Heart racing, she hopped from her car, leaving Matt's painting in the backseat, and ran to the front door.

The house was quiet and dark except for a small light in the kitchen. Aunt Erin and Stella often went to bed early so they could rise with the sun.

Romeo?

Camille tiptoed into the kitchen. Stella sat at the table alone with a steaming mug. Her eyes were red.

"Is everything all right?" Camille asked.

"Romeo came back. For the moment, yes, everything is all right."

Though she wanted to ask Stella where he was, she feared giving the woman an opportunity to scold her, to demand that she stay away. Perhaps Stella and Romeo should move out. This was Camille's house, too.

But what was she thinking? Camille shook her head. She had every intention of leaving, and Stella had come to live with Aunt Erin to keep her company. They needed each other.

Camille walked through the living room and the den then peered out the french doors to the deck and backyard. No Romeo.

Perhaps he didn't want to see her and had gone to bed. Camille climbed the stairs and headed for her office to shut down her computer. This would be another night she wouldn't read Shakespeare and wouldn't post on her blog. Would its growing popularity begin to die?

And. . . She needed to do something about the painting. But what?

Camille shoved through the door into the dark office. Moonlight streamed through the window, giving her attic an ethereal atmosphere.

The hair on the back of her arms quivered—someone else was in the room with her. She could feel it. In the far corner where darkness lingered, the silhouette of a man, sitting in the chair, sent her pulse hammering.

The intruder? No. . . Somehow, she knew. "Romeo?"

thirteen

Relieved to see he'd returned, Camille took a deep breath, trying to slow her racing heart. "Why are you sitting in the dark?" She reached for the light switch.

"Don't," he said, his voice throaty. "Leave the light off."

"Why?"

He rose from the chair and moved toward her. Was he still upset with her? "What are you doing?"

He came closer, silent. A shaft of moonlight flashed across his war-torn face. When he was less than a foot from her, he stopped. Even in the darkness, his presence overwhelmed her, made her light headed. The scent of his cologne mingled with leather.

"In the darkness, you can't see my scar. In the darkness, we're the same."

Camille's eyes welled. Trembling, she slid her hand to her throat. "Romeo," she whispered, "I never meant to hurt you."

"I know." He cupped her cheeks with his hands.

Camille savored his touch. Why was he being so tender? Didn't he hate her?

His face was mere inches from hers now. "You wanted to paint a portrait as a tribute to me. I understand that now. And. . .I'm honored."

Then Romeo's lips were on hers. Camille felt the emotion pouring from him, all the way to her toes. She slid her hands over his muscular chest, his broad shoulders, and up around his neck.

She could linger in Romeo's kiss, in his presence, forever. . . .

She sensed when he began to ease from the kiss—her lips already missed his tenderness.

Breathless, he pressed his forehead to hers. "Beautiful Camille, I've wanted to do that since the moment I met you."

"And what took you so long?"

"Because I wasn't sure. I didn't know how you felt."

Camille leaned forward and kissed him lightly. "And now that you do, why did you stop?"

Romeo sighed and drew away from her, if only a little. "Because you're a very passionate woman. I...I had to stop."

She pressed her head against his chest, loving the way she felt in his arms.

"And now is the time for you to show me the painting."

Camille pushed away from him to look in his eyes, but in the darkness, she couldn't see much at all. He was right. She couldn't see the scar and in a way, they were the same. She could pretend he was perfect. But did she want to?

"Romeo, I wanted to tell you. I tried to tell you, but there was never a good time, and then your mother..." *Oops.*

"My mother what?"

Romeo moved to the wall and flipped the lights on. "My mother what?"

Camille sagged. She always ruined everything. "She's right, you know. She told me how hurt you were over losing your fiancée. She reminded me that I have plans to leave. Romeo, she doesn't want to see you hurt again."

"She's not big on letting me make my own choices." Romeo paced, clearly irritated. "She has no right to interfere."

"What about what you said? That you want to be a good son."

"I came here with that intention, yes." Romeo closed the distance between them and took Camille's hands, bringing them to his lips. "I don't want to argue or talk about my mother."

Camille shook her head. "Neither do I." She smiled, basking in the attention he was giving her. He was so tender. She never expected this.

Kiss me again, Romeo. She leaned into him, expectantly. A girl could hope.

He pressed his lips against hers, softly this time, holding back the raw power and emotion she'd felt in the first kiss.

They could be so good together.

Pulling away, Romeo sighed. "Camille, I kissed you because, well. . .because I wanted to do that before I looked at the painting."

"What do you mean?"

"I have no idea what seeing it will do to me—how it will make me feel to see myself as I once was. Without a mutilated face." Romeo's voice broke. "I'm trying to get over it. I thought I had until I met you."

"But what does that have to do with kissing me?"

He twirled one of her obnoxious loose strands of hair in his fingers and grinned. The guy could make her float with a simple look. "Because I wanted you to know how I feel about you and that I appreciate what you were trying to do by painting me."

"You're afraid of your reaction?"

He nodded. "And then the moment to kiss you would be gone forever."

"I'm glad you kissed me first then." Camille feared this moment with him would pass too soon. "I'm going to ask you to wait a little longer."

Romeo sighed and frowned. "I need to see it tonight."

"But I know so much more about you. The painting, which is mostly ruined anyway, doesn't do you justice. Please pose for me, Romeo. Work with me, and I'll have a new painting ready in time to enter the competition."

Romeo's frown turned into a teasing smile. "When you say it like that, how can I resist?"

She could fall so hard for this guy.

"What's going on in here?" Stella stood in the doorway.

Romeo and Camille each took a step back as though

they'd been caught committing a crime. Camille should have expected Stella would find her way upstairs.

"It would be my honor to pose for your painting. Let's start tomorrow." He winked and walked toward his mother. "I'm talking to Camille about her painting. *Mama, perché sei interruzione.*"

"*Romeo, lei non è un bene per voi.*"

Their voices were loud but grew distant as they made their way down the stairs.

They speak Italian? "Huh." Camille sighed. She'd have to get him to talk to her in Italian. That would be so. . . romantic.

&

Rivulets of sweat slid down Romeo's back as he scraped the paint from the side of the house. His stomach growled. Was it lunchtime yet?

Mama hadn't wasted any time putting him on painting the big Victorian house—a home that didn't belong to her. He was sure she wanted to keep him occupied and away from Camille.

How was he supposed to research and do the legwork for getting a business started when Mama had such a long chore list?

I need to be a good son. But Mama made it difficult.

"*The girl is no good for you,*" she said last night. Her words kept him awake, conflicting with more pleasant thoughts of kissing Camille.

The way she'd responded. . . The kiss had been everything he imagined it could be and more.

What kind of man would he be to stand in the way of her dreams for an art degree at one of the top schools in the country? Yet he wasn't willing to give up what little time he might have with her. There was the other matter of the restaurant. Romeo wasn't entirely certain he wanted to start something here in town if Camille wasn't going to stay. The realization startled him—had he come to care for her so much already?

He couldn't convey any of this to Mama without getting into a heated argument. Her emotions raged out of control—like they had when Papa was alive. Rheumatoid arthritis didn't seem to dampen her harsh words at all. And every argument reminded him of the night he'd walked out and enlisted in the army.

Lord, what am I doing here? Romeo swiped the sweat from his forehead.

The sun had risen high in the sky. Surely it was time for lunch.

On top of the ladder, Romeo stretched over to scrape the last bit of paint on this section before heading to the kitchen in search of a sandwich. The scent of lilac drifted over him.

Camille. . .

He breathed the smell of her and smiled.

"I've come to rescue you." Her voice was melodic.

Romeo glanced down. "What makes you think I need rescuing?"

"Oh, just a hunch. Why paint when you could be painted?"

He wasn't exactly painting yet, but he wasn't about to argue the point. He didn't bother bringing up Mama and her temper. Camille would only remind him that he was a grown man.

"Is that from Shakespeare?" Romeo asked, climbing down the ladder.

Camille's laughter danced around him. "I see I have much to teach you."

When he stepped on the soft grass, Camille curtsied. "Our lesson begins tonight. I'll read Shakespeare to you and help you understand the Elizabethan English, and in return, you can speak to me in Italian."

Romeo burst out laughing.

"I didn't know until I heard you and your mother last

night." Camille leaned over to smell one of the azalea blooms. "I find it quite. . .appealing."

"Oh you do, do you?" Heat rose in Romeo's chest—he wasn't sure if he was blushing or something else.

"Speaking of appealing, before I paint you, let's get you fed and groomed."

Romeo chuckled. "What, you can't paint me like this?" He spread his arms out and gestured at his white T-shirt and khaki pants, covered with dirt and paint dust.

Her lips pressed into a wide smile. "Maybe next time."

Yes, and maybe next time they could have a serious discussion about where this flirtation was leading the both of them. For now, Romeo couldn't stop himself. Camille was the only light shining in the dark of his night. It scared him. . . .

But now that he'd met her—had kissed her—what would it be like to live without her? That's exactly what he might have to do if she left.

But on a day like today Romeo was happy to take what he could get.

With Camille, he forgot about his face. He brushed the back of his hand down the soft skin on her cheek and sighed, content, though worry remained at the edge of his thoughts.

"What's wrong?" Camille's eyes searched his.

She was too perceptive. How could he explain? After everything he'd been through, he wasn't sure he could give her the kind of love she deserved, wasn't sure he could open himself up to be loved. And maybe she wasn't even asking.

"Nothing," he said, tugging her close to kiss her forehead. "Let's eat."

fourteen

"Now, turn your face toward the light and lift your chin just so. Most portraits are a three-quarter view of the subject's profile," Camille said. "That will allow me to capture more definition of your facial features."

Romeo sat on a stool in the room that served as a small library. Walls of mahogany bookshelves surrounded her easel, canvas, and paint supplies. Sometimes the attic stifled her creativity.

"Now I'm going to take a snapshot just in case you change your mind."

Romeo opened his mouth to speak.

"Ah, don't move." Camille lifted her camera and gazed through the lens. She'd positioned a lamp with a hundred-watt bulb about five feet away from him. The difference between the light and the dark side of his face would translate into a three-dimensional picture on canvas. A good portion of his scar was shadowed.

"But how many days do you have before this needs to be done?"

"No talking." She focused on his face. "Say cheese. . . . Scratch that. Look solemn and. . .heroic."

Romeo's eyes cast off troubled emotions. Were unbidden memories accosting him? Then his eyes cleared and admiration drifted into his gentle gaze. Camille smiled and took the shot.

She chuckled. Assuming he couldn't tolerate posing for long—it was sometimes difficult for children and men to sit still—Camille got right to work. She took some burnt sienna, mixed it with turpentine to make a lighter, more transparent brown, and marked the canvas to shape Romeo's face. After lightly shaping the forehead and eyebrows and putting dimension in the nose, Camille focused on where to place the opening of his mouth. Thoughts of his kiss rose in her mind.

The temperature in the small room had risen another ten degrees, she was sure. As Romeo stared into the distance, she was grateful he wasn't able to read her mind, or she'd never finish this painting.

She worked intently and knew from experience that time would pass quickly for her but slowly for him. When Romeo began fidgeting, Camille glanced at the small clock she'd put out of his line of vision.

"Oh come on, you've only been here half an hour."

Romeo looked stricken. "Is that all?"

"Go ahead and talk to me, if that will keep you occupied. I can still work."

"What do you want to hear?"

The structure of his face laid out on canvas, Camille began blending the paint colors on the palette to create Romeo's skin tones. "Tell me about growing up in an Italian restaurant, about Afghanistan—I don't know. Whatever you want to talk about."

Romeo stared at her.

Though Camille didn't want to disturb his pose, she put her paintbrush down and moved around the easel. Standing in front of him, she leaned forward and planted a soft kiss on his lips. "I want to know everything about you, Romeo," she whispered. "Start from the beginning."

He cleared his throat. She made him nervous. Cute.

She moved back to her place in front of the canvas and started working again.

"Did you know I had a brother?" he asked, his tone a little too solemn.

Camille stopped painting. *Had?*

Maybe it wouldn't be so easy to paint if he was going to throw that kind of news at her. She frowned and tried to focus again. "No, I didn't."

"He was killed in a car accident," he said. His expression turned dark and brooding.

Camille didn't interrupt. She wanted to hear more, hoping she would be able to portray the emotion pouring from him. But it was never that easy. Some paintings were inspired—only God knew why.

Lord, please help me honor this soldier. Help me to depict all that is this man on the canvas.

She sensed Romeo was a complex man, and she hadn't come close to knowing who he really was. And, with her prayer, she realized she was asking this in part to honor Romeo, yes, but also to create a winning portrait.

Winning would mean leaving the man she admired. A man she wanted to be with. How could she reconcile her two desires?

"Emilio was the one Papa groomed to take over the family business. He *wanted* to run it. I didn't. When he died, I not only lost a brother. I lost my freedom, my choice." He knitted his brows.

Maybe getting him to talk wasn't a good idea. Didn't he have any pleasant memories?

"I always felt like Papa wished I was the one who died instead. I argued with Mama and Papa the night I left the kitchen. For all the wrong reasons, I ended up enlisting in the army. While I was away Papa died." He paused, swallowing. "I'm proud to have served. I just wished I could have done so under different circumstances."

Camille's vision blurred. She knew exactly what it was like to feel second best.

She put down the paintbrush and rushed to Romeo, pulling him to his feet. She tugged his head down to hers and kissed him, desperate to make his pain go away. She felt so sorry for all his suffering, but she was hardly adequate to bring healing to his soul—only God could do that.

Why was she trying?

&

Romeo couldn't respond to Camille's kiss, not like he'd done before. He held her at arm's length.

"I don't want your pity, Camille." He searched her eyes, seeing confusion there.

She shook her head. "Pity is the last thing I'd ever have for you."

Camille looked openly at his scar, and he saw respect in her eyes—not the usual loathing and disgust he'd seen in so many others. But was this all about the scar to her?

He released her and turned his back, searching for the words. "No, you don't pity me. But I have to wonder. . ." Romeo turned to face her again. "Camille, are you sure you aren't romanticizing my disfigurement?"

Her eyebrows scrunched together. "I don't know what you mean."

"I never thought I'd be saying this, but would you care about me if I didn't have this souvenir from the war?" Romeo couldn't help the nervous laugh that escaped, but he was beginning to hear wisdom in Mama's words. Camille was simply infatuated with him because of his military service, because of his injury. Her hopes and dreams lay elsewhere.

Hurt flickered in her eyes before she averted her gaze. She stepped away from him and ran her fingers across a few books on the shelf, disturbing a layer of dust. If it hadn't been for Mama's arthritis, she would have seen to that by now. Erin obviously wasn't as meticulous about housework.

"Romeo, what I feel for you—it's very real to me. But how can a person know if what they're feeling is not simply infatuation? How do you know if what you feel for *me* is real?"

Romeo's spirits slumped. He couldn't believe anyone could

love him. He'd dared to hope with Camille, even in the face of knowing her dreams could lead her somewhere far from him.

Grit seemed to fill his mouth as he considered his answer. When Camille gave up wiping dust from the books to look his way again, a tear hung from her lashes. She took a few steps and laid her face against his chest. Wrapping his arms around her, he savored the feeling of being needed.

"I think that whatever is between us could grow into something wonderful. Something powerful," she said, her voice muffled against his shirt.

"I know." He kissed the top of her head, inhaling the lilac in her hair. "Me, too."

Camille stepped back. "Why does it have to be so hard?"

"Because neither one of us were expecting this. We hadn't planned for it. You have goals and dreams. I don't want to stand in the way of those."

She scraped loose strands of her wild, curly hair back and repinned them. "And I don't want to hurt you."

Romeo hated hearing the despondency in her voice. When he'd first met her, she was lighthearted and happy.

"Then we need to take things much slower."

She toyed with her paintbrushes, and he smiled a little at her familiar habit. Just as she reached for another brush, he put his hand over hers and squeezed. "Camille," he whispered. "Look at me."

She squeezed her eyes shut then opened them again before looking up to him.

"Maybe if I hadn't kissed you that night. . ."

"Don't. I wanted the kiss. Tell me, Romeo, how do we go back? How do we slow things down?"

He sighed. "I don't know."

Camille moved away from Romeo to stand on the other side of the canvas. She angled her head slightly, looking back and forth between the painting and Romeo. "I still have a lot of detail to add, but we can take a break for now."

Oh great, I get to go scrape paint. Romeo accepted that he'd been dismissed, but he wasn't sure where that left things between them.

He changed back into his painting clothes and noticed he had a call on his cell. He sighed, knowing Kent was expecting an answer. But Romeo was in no frame of mind to discuss the future—too much was unsettled. He'd give him a call back later tonight and ask for more time to make his decision.

As he climbed up the ladder, Erin pulled into the driveway with Mama. The women exited the vehicle, and Mama waved and made her way over to him.

Hands on her hips, she stared up at him, shielding her eyes from the sun. "You haven't made much progress."

Romeo ignored her comment. "What did the doctor say? Did he adjust your medication?"

"No. He told me to give this new stuff some time."

He made his way down the ladder and stood on the last rung. "But you're feeling better, aren't you? You've been planting flowers like crazy."

Mama nodded and smiled. "It was just a checkup. You should be grateful Erin took me, or else you would have been stuck with the job."

"That I am." He winked.

"But why haven't you been working?"

"I had to pose for Camille's painting, Mama. I told you about that."

Her lips compressed. "What about the restaurant? Have you given it any thought?"

Romeo stepped onto the grass and began gathering his tools. He recognized how patient she'd been, not questioning him. But something had set her off. "Yes, and I'm still thinking on it."

She patted his shoulder. "I love you, my Romeo."

He hated that she never called him her handsome Romeo anymore.

"I met a nice young woman at the doctor's office. I invited her over for dinner tonight."

How dare she? Was she that desperate to get him away from Camille? Romeo wasn't ready to face the scrutiny.

"Did you explain that your son was mutilated in Afghanistan?" It took everything in him to keep the venom from his words.

"Telling her that would only scare her off before she had a chance to meet you and decide for herself. You are still the most handsome young man I know. Surely, given Camille's attentions, you know this."

He ground his teeth to keep from speaking his mind. It would only end in an argument. Erin came to stand beside his mother and gave him a look that said she understood his dilemma.

"I won't be here. I've already made plans for dinner," he said. He'd come up with something.

fifteen

Camille was accustomed to taking her time when painting, taking days and even weeks, depending on the complexity and intricacy of detail, until she finally decided her work was finished. With the contest looming, she didn't have that kind of time. Her portrait had to be in the Redwood Art Association's offices no later than Friday—just two days away.

Romeo had returned to scraping paint from the house, preparing it for a new coat. He'd left her to finish what she could on the portrait without him, but she had a copy of the digital photo. Her main concern was never about the technical aspects—her rendering would be accurate. But Camille's goal was deeper. The image she created should be more than a precise depiction. It should convey emotion and touch the heart of the beholder.

She inhaled and took a step back to look at her progress. At first glance, yes, she had definitely captured the image of Romeo, though she needed to add detail—much more detail.

And the emotion? What exactly was the painting saying to her? An ache sliced through her heart.

After their emotionally charged discussion—about where their relationship was headed and just how fast—there was no way for her to be objective about her painting now. She'd have to give it a break, put her thoughts on something entirely different, and come back later for a second look.

While cleaning her brushes, she thought about how Aunt Erin wouldn't care about the smell of oil paint and turpentine in the house. But Stella might have a few words to say. Camille almost snickered.

The woman had changed since Romeo's arrival, especially

in her attitude toward Camille. One of the most interesting changes was her slip back into her painful display of rheumatoid arthritis. Camille thought she'd finally found a medication to ease her pain. She seemed to be doing well— until Romeo showed up.

Was it simply a coincidence, or did his presence affect her in such a way that her RA flared up? Was Stella putting on an act to gain Romeo's attention and sympathy, to keep him here?

Camille hated herself for even considering the thought.

No matter. She had plans that would take her far from here.

And Romeo. . .

Why, God? Why is this happening? Just when things were beginning to go her way, this amazing man came into her life and threw her plans off.

Heading upstairs to clean her room, Camille prayed silently. *Lord, I'm doing my best here. I know that if it's Your will for me to fulfill my dreams of getting that art degree, then You'll work things out. I'll win the contest. And if it's not. . .*

Camille shoved through the door of her room. *And if it's not?* She could hardly bear to consider that possibility, and yet part of her wasn't even sure what she really wanted. Success, ambition—all those things reminded her of Alexa. Camille had to wonder, if Alexa hadn't left Northern California to make something of herself, would Camille be trying?

Why did it matter so much to her what Alexa thought?

And what about her newfound feelings for Romeo?

Hadn't finding love also been a dream? A dream she'd shoved to the deepest corner of her heart?

After washing her hands and face, Camille slipped on a clean shirt. The aroma of fish wafted under the door. Dinner would be ready by now. She placed her hand on the doorknob, and someone knocked.

Her heart leaped. Romeo? She opened the door.

"I brought dinner up to you," Aunt Erin said, holding a

plate of fish, English peas, and rice. "Thought you might be hungry."

That's unusual. "Oh? I was just on my way down."

Aunt Erin practically forced her way into the room, and Camille stepped out of her path.

"I think it's best if you eat in your room tonight." She set the plate on Camille's desk.

Camille was certain her mouth slid open—she'd never eaten in her room since coming to live here. "What's going on? Is it Stella?"

Aunt Erin sagged onto the bed. "Oh, Stella invited a girl she met at the doctor's office over for dinner tonight, hoping to set her up with Romeo. Romeo wasn't happy to hear the news and said he had other plans. Stella tried to call the girl but couldn't get an answer. I have no idea if she'll show up or not. I just don't want you to have to deal with the friction, and honestly, I'm too tired to deal with it myself."

Camille wrapped her arms around herself, smiling. "So Romeo wasn't going to lie down and take it."

"I have eyes like Stella. I see you're infatuated with her son. Don't let him railroad plans that will take you places. Don't forget all I've taught you, Camille—you don't need a man. Look at your sister, Sela. She got married, and he died. Now she's stuck running that shop and barely making ends meet. Besides, if you and Romeo end up getting married, Stella would have a conniption fit. I'm here to tell you she'd cause you a lot of problems. Would you really want a mother-in-law like that?"

Really? You, too, Aunt Erin? Why were both women so against love between her and Romeo, of a possible future for them? Camille couldn't find the words to respond, nor was she certain she wanted to miss the dinner downstairs.

Aunt Erin walked over to the window and tugged the drapes aside, staring out. Probably watching for Stella's dinner guest.

Just the mention of marriage to Romeo sent Camille's heart floating. But the thought of Stella working so hard to keep them apart quickly landed her feet on the ground. If Stella was that intent on bringing home every girl she met to entice Romeo, how long would he last before succumbing?

Aunt Erin sighed. "Well, I had better go down and find out what's happening. Wouldn't want to make Stella eat alone if the girl doesn't show."

Just before Camille closed the door behind Aunt Erin, she took one step back into the room. "Stay away from him just a little longer, okay? I have a feeling he'll be moving along soon anyway."

"I'll try." Was she beaten at every turn?

She took a seat at the desk, picked up her fork, and stabbed at her fish, but her appetite had left the room with Aunt Erin.

Why should she care if Romeo left? She planned to leave, didn't she? Camille laid the fork and knife across the plate for now and lay on her bed, suddenly feeling very tired. Where had Romeo gone tonight?

Camille woke up and realized she'd fallen asleep. She pushed up on her elbows and looked around the room. It had grown dark outside. Her clock said 9:30. What happened at dinner? Did the girl come over? She spotted the plate of fish on her desk. Her room would stink for a week.

She grabbed the plate to deliver it to the kitchen. Tonight would be a good night to catch up on reading Shakespeare. She glanced at her nightstand. The script of *Much Ado about Nothing* wasn't there. It must be in the living room, where she hoped to read it with Romeo later.

Downstairs in the kitchen, she dumped the food in the garbage and rinsed the plate. The dishwasher was already running, so she left it in the sink. Camille crept down the hall, past the library and her unfinished painting, and toward the living room.

Romeo's voice spoke in low tones from the room. Perhaps the girl had come after all, and Romeo had stayed. Camille's heart sank. She turned to go back but remembered her script. Would it be rude to interrupt them and grab the Shakespeare play from the coffee table?

Uncertain what to do, Camille stood outside the doorway against the wall and listened in, just for a second, to get a sense of what was going on.

"I told you I needed a few weeks to see my mother, then I should be there."

The room fell silent.

"I'll talk to you in a few days."

So. . . Romeo had his own plans to leave, after all. It was just as Aunt Erin suspected. Camille almost sank to her knees at the news. How could she convince him to stay? She wasn't even a consideration in his plans. No wonder he'd suggested they take things slow—in fact, why bother even entertaining a romantic relationship? Where could it possibly lead?

She stood tall and wiped away the moisture at the corners of her eyes. Shoving herself away from the wall, she started into the living room to grab her script and leave, but in the doorway, she hung back.

Romeo sat in the chair reading the play. At the sight, warmth spread through her, heating up the cold toward him that threatened moments before.

❧

Romeo stared at the words on the page. For the life of him he couldn't understand them—but Camille loved Shakespeare. He had to reread the page several times because he honestly couldn't focus on the words. Too many thoughts were battling for his attention.

"Maybe if I hadn't kissed you that night." His earlier words to Camille wouldn't just fade away into oblivion. Even if given the chance, he wouldn't take back the kiss—in it he'd

found everything he wanted.

He pinched the bridge of his nose as though he could shut off the flow of emotions. He wished now that he hadn't suggested they take things slower. He would give anything to make her love him, to have her stay. But that wasn't love. Not really.

And just like he'd set Maria free, breaking off their engagement, he cared for Camille enough to do the same. Anything else would be selfish, and in the end, he feared she'd resent him.

He opened his eyes, thinking if he kept reading it would bring him closer to Camille somehow. Something stirred in his peripheral vision.

Camille leaned against the door frame, her skirt of yellow and blue flowers wrapped around her legs. The simple sight of her slim form, the soft expression on her face, stirred him.

How much of this could he take? Maybe he should just move on down the road to the job that waited for him. There was no getting around the pain of falling for a woman he knew he couldn't have—but. . . He just couldn't leave her. Not yet.

"Camille," he said, his voice a whisper. He placed the script on the side table and leaned forward.

Something behind her eyes had changed. "I see you found the script. I was looking for it." She took it and thumbed through the pages. "I saw you reading it."

Romeo leaned back in the chair and laughed. "I'm not sure that's what you would call it. I couldn't understand a thing. Why don't we read it together?"

That finally brought a smile to her face, but it didn't reach her eyes. "Can I give you a rain check? I really need to spend some time blogging tonight. I've neglected that for too many days now."

"And that makes a difference?"

"Yes." She shrugged. "I don't know why. I guess if people

are expecting to read something they'll stop by, but if you slack off, then you lose readers."

"Well, I guess you'd better get busy writing."

Camille toyed with the script and frowned. "Maybe tomorrow night I can read to you if you still want me to."

"Sounds like a plan. Tonight we'll work on your blog."

Her eyes grew wide, and she huffed. "*We?*"

"I've wanted to read your blog since I heard about it."

"Romeo." Again the sigh. "I overheard you talking on your cell."

He didn't reply. He wanted to hear what exactly she heard. What she would say next.

Camille sank on the sofa across from him. "I think I understand better now why you wanted us to take things slowly. You're planning to leave. There's no future for us anyway."

He squeezed his eyes closed, thinking about how best to explain. The last thing he wanted was to throw an even bigger obstacle between them. Eyes still closed, he inhaled slowly then released the breath.

"Camille." He opened his eyes. "You only heard part of the conversation. My plans are not set in stone. And as for our future, I wish that I hadn't said the words, hadn't said we need to take things slowly."

"There's a *but*, isn't there?"

"Yes. You already know. You have plans to leave, too."

Camille stared at the script.

"Today while I posed for you, I watched you working on the portrait. You were so passionate, and there was a light in your eyes. Your face came alive. I've never seen you look so beautiful." He huffed out a breath. "That confirmed to me how much you want to win, how much you need this. This is your dream."

"You're right." Looking at the script, avoiding Romeo's eyes, Camille rose from the sofa. "It is."

sixteen

Romeo wasn't sure how it happened, but somehow the decision to take things slower had translated into complete avoidance. Maybe two people who were powerfully drawn to one another weren't capable of mere friendship.

All he knew was that if it was painful to be with her, knowing that he could lose her any moment, it was even more painful to be apart. Definitely he should never have kissed her, should never have crossed that line into a full-blown romantic relationship. It was as though a simple kiss had sealed his heart to hers. Now only one question remained—had it sealed his fate to hers, too?

Sitting in a corner at the little Internet café, Romeo wished the lighting was much darker. Why didn't Bernardino's have wireless access? Maybe if he bought the place or started up his own, he'd offer free Internet. He'd had to leave the house because he didn't want Mama asking questions—she'd immediately put him to work, especially if she knew what he was up to.

Coming here at all, being seen in public, had been a huge step for him, but he was a desperate man, and in a way, his desperation helped him put aside self-consciousness.

He tugged the baseball cap lower, hoping he would simply fade into the woodwork. So far, only a few had paid him any attention—the usual look of surprise then averting the eyes, embarrassment, pity, and disgust written across their faces.

As he waited for his new laptop to power up, he considered the last few days. He'd posed for Camille one last time for a strained and awkward couple of hours. Then she didn't even let him see the finished painting, pleading with him to wait.

Wait for what?

Now a portrait of him was in the hands of the Redwood Art Association. Would he ever see what she thought of him? Maybe she feared if he saw the painting, he wouldn't allow it to be displayed. At the thought, Romeo tugged his cap a little lower.

He hoped to find some answers in her blog. Maybe he could understand a little bit of her thinking. If nothing else, he wanted to feel close to her again.

Once his laptop connected with the café's wifi, Camille's *In Love with Shakespeare* blog came up at the top of his search results.

Seeing it for the first time eased his mind. This was almost like spending time with her, and in some odd way—he allowed himself a grin—it made him feel more connected to her.

Romeo ordered a caramel macchiato and searched through the blog posts for the first one. Finding it, he took a scalding sip of his coffee and leaned back in the chair.

A smile came to his lips.

I'm intrigued with Shakespeare's portrayal of human passion ranging from hate and murder to love and sacrifice. I don't claim to be an expert—I'm just a beginner. Why not join me in my quest to learn more? Together we can discover truths about human nature as portrayed by Shakespeare.

Romeo was completely drawn in as he read post after post, many of them titled with modern-day sayings attributed to Shakespeare. He could hear her whimsical voice as though she read each post to him. The readers wrote enthusiastic comments about Camille's insights. Camille would respond, turning things into a lively and healthy discussion.

As the hours passed, Romeo found himself nearing the more current posts. Her tone began to change. He took a drink from the coffee cup, and cold liquid met his lips.

At the beginning she sounded like someone who was eager

to grow and excited about life. But now she seemed cautious and wary. Romeo sat.

He continued reading. One of the blog comments was posted by a Don John. *Your beauty which did haunt me in my sleep could make me undertake the death of all the world.*

It sounded like it was directed at Camille herself. She had an admirer. Jealousy swarmed Romeo. Of course, she must have many men who were interested. But this was disturbing.

Scrolling down further, Romeo again found a post from Don John. The man mentioned he'd seen her around town and thought she was beautiful.

Did she know this guy personally? Who was Don John?

Finally, Romeo scrolled to Camille's post from last night, after he'd seen her in the living room.

She titled it, "To Be or Not to Be." Camille wrote, *I know I'm dropping* Hamlet *into our discussion, so I hope you'll forgive my diversion. My understanding is that Hamlet's soliloquy is regarding revenge, but how many times have you heard this phrase in your lifetime? Have you ever applied it to your life? That's what I'm doing now, and in fact, I'm expanding. I'm considering whether to be loved or to not be loved. . . .*

Romeo tensed. Did she have any idea he would read her blog? He asked her about reading it last night, but she refused to allow him to see. Just like she refused to let him see the painting.

Romeo skimmed the comments to see if Don John had anything to say on the matter.

Good that you're discussing Hamlet now. "Soft you now! The fair Ophelia—Nymph, in thy orisons be all my sins remembered."

Romeo wasn't exactly sure what that meant, but he intended to ask Camille. He had a bad feeling about the whole thing.

❧

At five thirty, Camille stood outside Mary's Curio Shop as Mary locked up. Mary had invited her to stop by at the end of the day to think up new items she could make, since her purses were really taking off.

Mary turned the key in the lock. "So, business is good, and I expect things to pick up with the art fair and exhibit starting next week. Tourists go crazy."

"As agreed, I'll start increasing the number of bags I bring and come up with a few new items. But you know—"

"If you win, you're probably out of here." Mary tugged her bag—one of Camille's—over her shoulder. "You know, kiddo, I'll be sorry to see you go. People will be clamoring for your designs."

"Oh Mary." Camille frowned. "I hope I haven't put you into a bad position. Thanks so much for believing in me and giving me a chance."

"There really wasn't a choice to make—your work is amazing. No matter what you put your hand to, Camille, you're going to succeed. Just remember that, even if you don't win this contest."

Camille cocked her head. "You know something I don't?"

Mary laughed. "Don't read between the lines. You're far too sensitive. You want to know a secret? That sister of yours has got nothing on you."

"You really think so?" Camille smiled, loving the compliment, but she didn't believe it.

"I really think so." Mary winked at Camille then looked both ways and took a step off the curb.

"Have a great weekend, Mary. And thanks." Camille watched her cross the street and head to the small parking lot between the shops. Before she climbed into her car, she gave Camille a little wave.

Camille sighed. What she needed right now was a cup of strong coffee before she headed home to make dinner. She was already running a little late on that task. She strolled down the sidewalk to the little coffeehouse just up the way. What did Mary mean? Did she think Camille was in some big competition with Alexa? She hated that Mary could see through her like that.

"Camille," a man said from behind.

She whirled to see Matt grinning at her.

"Fancy seeing you here," he said.

"Yeah, imagine that." Camille smiled and hoped he would go away. He was a nice guy, but he just rubbed her the wrong way. She didn't know what it was about Matt, but lately. . .

"How about dinner?"

Unable to think of a response, Camille stared at Matt, searching for an excuse.

"Or I can just walk with you."

"I. . .uh. . . You don't have to do that."

Matt sagged. "No, it's all right. Let's go."

He took off in the direction she had been walking and looked back expectantly.

Camille didn't know what else to do, so she walked alongside him. But she could sense his demeanor had changed from pleasant surprise to something sour.

"Where did you end up hanging my painting?" he asked.

Panic raked over her—she'd not even taken it from the backseat. She certainly couldn't allow him to walk her to her car. Maybe she would be forced to have that coffee with him after all.

"I haven't decided yet. It's beautiful, Matt. Thank you." Matt was a good-looking man. He could probably pick any woman he wanted, except for Camille. Why didn't she like him? Why did Romeo stir her senses, her soul? Romeo—a man with baggage and a million issues he hadn't dealt with. Why did she have to be drawn to him?

As they approached the coffee shop, she hesitated. Should she go inside? She couldn't be rude if Matt insisted on joining her. She'd wanted a few minutes of peace before heading home to start dinner.

Matt put his hand on the doorknob, leaning toward her. "Join me for a cup of coffee at least?"

"There you are," Romeo said, sliding his hand around Camille's waist.

Though stunned by his sudden appearance, Camille realized Romeo was trying to help. "Matt, this is Romeo. We're having coffee together. Would you like to join us?"

Matt looked at Romeo's scar and scowled at him.

Her chest ached. What a jerk.

"No thanks. Maybe some other time," Matt said.

While Matt hurried across the street corner, Camille allowed herself to be escorted into the café. She exhaled, shoulders unknotting, and turned to Romeo. "How. . . How did you know?"

Romeo tugged his red baseball cap lower and led her to a back corner. He pulled out a chair for her and sat across from her. He leaned forward on his elbows. "You had that look on your face that said you wished he would go away."

"So you made him go away." Matt's behavior depressed her. Had he left because of Romeo's scar? Was that how Romeo saw it? Or had he left because Camille had plans with Romeo?—which she hadn't had until that moment.

She hoped for the latter but couldn't help but wonder how different her life would be if she had to cope with the things Romeo had to deal with every day. "Thank you," she whispered. He'd risked Matt's scorn for her. She could have excused herself by simply informing Matt it was her night to make dinner, but that thought had slipped her mind completely when he startled her.

"I'm just glad you're having coffee with me instead of him." Romeo slipped his hand across the table and covered hers. "How about dinner at Bernardino's?"

Something tingled inside Camille. Was he asking her on a date? "Tonight's my night to cook, and I'm late as it is. I wanted to grab a cup of coffee for the drive home."

"Instead you're sitting here with me." Romeo's gaze teased her tangled heart.

"I'm sitting here with you," she said.

"How about we cook together? I'm not sure why I didn't think of that earlier. I should do some of the cooking, if not all." He grinned.

She was growing to love his quirky grin, set off just a bit by damaged skin.

"We'd better grab our coffee to go then."

Just when she thought they had agreed to slow the pace, a rush of crazy emotions—excitement, attraction, and something much deeper and more meaningful—flip-flopped inside her.

Oh Lord, what am I going to do?

A switch from Shakespeare to Song of Solomon would probably be appropriate if she continued down this path. From the first moment she'd met him, Romeo had changed everything for her—even inspiring the painting for the very contest that could send her away from him.

With the art festival beginning tomorrow, the next few days would be the proving ground. Would she win? She'd pinned so much hope—her future, in fact—on this.

seventeen

Standing in the kitchen over steaming pots of marinara and pesto sauce, pans of penne and spaghetti, Camille had to wipe her brow with the back of her hand.

Of course, Romeo was doing most of the cooking, but he'd set her to work stirring the sauces and watching the pasta.

He appeared to her left, dumping more sautéed garlic and onions into his sauce. He bumped her elbow.

Camille giggled. "Don't you think the kitchen is too small for two cooks?"

"That depends on the cooks." He gave her a mischievous look that made her toes tingle. "But if you'll tell me your secret ingredient, I'll let you join your aunt and my mother on the deck."

"What, and leave you to take all the credit?" She elbowed him back. "Forget about it."

He laughed then lifted a wooden spoon to taste the sauce. For a few seconds, his expression was thoughtful, then he frowned. "This doesn't come close to yours."

"Let me taste." She leaned toward the bubbling pot as Romeo held a spoonful for her. Careful not to burn herself, Camille blew on it then pressed her mouth over the spoon.

She closed her eyes and savored the flavor. "I don't know. It's not the same, but it certainly rivals mine."

When she looked up, Romeo was staring at her, admiration in his eyes. Heat warmed her cheeks from the inside—they were certainly hot enough hovering over the stove—and she turned her attention to the pasta rippling in the boiling water. "I think it's ready. Should I call them?"

If she leaned back just so, she could see past the fridge and out the large bay window in the dining room where the two women sat enjoying peppermint tea. *Ugh.* Just then they stood.

"Looks like they can smell that dinner is ready," Romeo said.

The table in the dining room was already set with place settings. Camille and Romeo began draining pasta and shoveling it into serving dishes. She took the garlic french bread from the oven and sliced it.

Aunt Erin stood in the opening between the kitchen and dining room, tugging off her wide-brimmed hat. "Smells like a fine Italian restaurant in here. You need any help?"

"I think we've got it." Camille finished slicing the bread. "Go wash up then take a seat at the table. We're almost done."

Camille allowed herself a glance at Romeo. He circled the dining table, setting the various dishes on either end, wearing a big white apron. He looked content—happier than she'd ever seen him.

As if he'd sensed her watching, he glanced her way and held her gaze for a second. "Could you bring that extra bowl of marinara sauce, Camille?"

She grabbed pot holders and lifted the pan.

Aunt Erin hung her garden hat on the rack. "Oh, Camille! I forgot to tell you. Alexa called. She and Sela are headed this way tomorrow. They want to tour the art festival and see your painting."

The words seemed to hit Camille in slow motion. Aunt Erin stared, as did Romeo and Stella. Their mouths hung open.

She heard their cries as the pot of marinara slipped from her fingers.

The pan fell to the floor with a resounding *clang*. Red tomato sauce exploded across the white kitchen tiles.

Camille stood frozen as she stared in horror at the tomato-y mess. She held her hands out. "Oh! I'm so sorry."

Tears filled her eyes, and her chin quivered. She'd ruined dinner, and. . . "Alexa and Sela are coming?"

Before she could react, Romeo was by her side. He turned her to face him. "It's all right. I'll clean it up. You go. Sit. Eat."

She stared at his lips moving, struggling to comprehend his words.

Aunt Erin grabbed a roll of paper towels from the counter. "Whatever is the matter with you?" She stood next to Romeo but directed her words at Camille.

&

Romeo wiped sauce from Camille's face, marveling that she seemed not to notice. He wanted to laugh the moment off, but Camille's demeanor sobered him up.

Erin snapped her fingers in Camille's face. "Snap out of it, girl."

Camille's eyes widened. "Sorry, I. . . Why are they coming again?"

"For the art exhibit. To see your painting, of course."

Finally, Camille joined Erin and Romeo in wiping up the mess.

"Ladies, please." Romeo grabbed each of them by the arm and dragged them to the dining room. "Let's eat, then I'll clean up the mess. I offered to cook, so the kitchen is mine." He tried to ease the tension in the room with a smile. "Mama has witnessed plenty of debacles in her restaurant days, haven't you, Mama?"

Mama gave him a look that told him she wanted to clobber Camille over the head with a pan. Romeo stared at her, pleading for her agreement.

She waved her hand. "Honestly, I don't know what all the fuss is about. Let Romeo take care of it. He'll have it cleaned up in no time."

He almost sagged with relief. Once Camille was seated— still looking uncertain—he busied himself serving the others. He hoped they would talk more about Camille's sisters. He wanted to understand her negative reaction, but Mama and Erin started a conversation about a UPS delivery of gardening tools they were expecting.

He'd forgotten just how much he enjoyed the cooking and serving it up. Why hadn't he considered doing this from the beginning? Perhaps this was how Camille felt when she found her inspiration for painting.

Once the ladies were served and busy eating, he wiped the kitchen down as quickly as possible. He hoped he'd finish in time to join them, because he wanted to gauge their reactions to his cooking. But by the time he slid into the chair across from Camille, forks were lying on the plates—except for Camille's.

Erin leaned back in her chair and looked at him. "I don't think you need Camille's secret ingredient, Romeo. This was wonderful. Thank you."

"What time?" Camille asked, staring at her untouched plate.

Mama and Erin studied her.

"What time what?" Erin asked.

"What time will they be here?" Camille toyed with her food, much like he'd seen her toy with her paintbrushes.

"Sela is picking Alexa up at the airport in the morning. Then they'll head this way. So, I'm guessing about noon." Erin reached across the table and placed her hand on Camille's. "I thought you'd be excited to see them."

Camille grinned a little. "I am. I'm just. . .surprised, that's all."

"You're afraid you won't live up to Alexa's expectations." Erin offered an apologetic look at Romeo and Mama.

Camille gave a nervous laugh, looking around the table. "I don't think we need to air all the family laundry, Aunt Erin."

"You're right." Erin started collecting dishes. "Forgive me. Sometimes I speak before I think."

Romeo rose as well. "Let me get that."

"You cooked. I'll clean." Apparently Erin was going to fight over the dishes.

She wasn't going to win against Romeo. He took the dishes from her. "I enjoy it. It reminds me of when I was growing up."

He tossed a smile Mama's way. She appeared pleased. The sooner he could get the kitchen cleaned up, the sooner he could get to the bottom of Camille's relationship with her sisters. And there was the matter of the blog comments. He'd wanted to bring that up at the coffee shop, but it hadn't been the right time.

A half hour later, he had his hands in soapy dishwater—the dishwasher wasn't big enough for so many pots and pans—and reached up to scratch his nose with the back of his hand.

"Need some help?" Camille stood next to him, smiling up. "I mean with your nose, not the dishes."

He laughed. "Were you waiting for me to finish before you offered to help?"

She tilted her head. "I thought you insisted on doing this yourself."

"I did, but an offer of help is always nice." He flicked water at her.

"Hey!" She wiped the bubbles from her face.

Romeo appreciated how he could be himself with her, how he'd lost his self-consciousness. How could he allow her to slip away from him? But he couldn't stop her, nor should he. If she stayed, it would be because she wanted to stay. Not because he'd pressured her or enticed her.

Standing next to him, she dried the dishes. Her perfume mingled with the scent of the dishwashing soap, stirring his memory of their first kiss.

He wanted to kiss her now. But they had agreed to slow down. And he had yesterday's blog post to think about.

"To be loved or not to be loved. . ."

He scrubbed another pan, rubbing as hard as he could.

Camille pressed her hand over his. "Careful now, you're going to kill that pan."

He rinsed the soap away, avoiding her eyes. "I read your blog today."

eighteen

Camille was suddenly desperate for a glass of water, tea. . . anything. She grabbed the pitcher of peppermint tea still sitting on the counter and poured a glass then took a long drink.

Romeo watched her. He scrunched up his face, giving it a comical look. She was sure his reaction was due to her contortions as she struggled to swallow. She couldn't very well spit the tea out in front of him.

"This stuff is awful." She wiped her mouth then poured the rest down the sink.

Romeo chuckled, finished drying the last pan, and stuck it away in the cabinet. "Did you hear what I said?"

"Yes." And she wasn't sure what to think. That last post. Why had she written it? Didn't she realize that Romeo would read her blog? "How did you. . . When. . .?"

Did he crack the password on the computer in the attic? Camille set the tea glass on the counter a little too hard.

"Don't look so surprised. I bought a laptop and went to an Internet café. Started reading at the beginning." He tugged the apron off and laid it on the counter.

"You did?"

Romeo inhaled then released the breath. "As much as I love the kitchen, maybe we can talk about this somewhere else?"

Aunt Erin's and Stella's laughter reached them from the living room, where the two women watched *Wheel of Fortune*.

Camille wanted to go somewhere more private with Romeo, but she wasn't all that certain she wanted to talk about that blog post. She should just delete it, but then her readers would want to know why.

Being near him like this, all she wanted was to be in his arms. Except, with their uncertain futures, she didn't want to hurt Romeo. Was it already too late for the both of them?

"I thought we agreed to take things slowly," Camille said. It was one thing to cook dinner together, but another to go somewhere together, especially when all she wanted was to kiss him again.

Camille shoved away from the kitchen counter. She felt certain her heart would break if they were to part. And yet, she could realize her dream in a few days, a dream that would take her away from. . . She stared at Romeo. What if. . . What if she gave up her plans and stayed to find out if they had a future together, and in the end, they didn't?

"How about sitting on the deck where your aunt and my mother can see us?" He offered his hand.

"Romeo, look, I'm really tired, and tomorrow the art festival starts, and my sisters—"

"I know, I know. Your sisters are coming. Mind telling me why that bothers you so much?"

Camille's mouth dropped open. "What makes you think that?"

"After the marinara incident, your feelings about them aren't exactly a secret." Romeo withdrew his hand and ran it through his thick, dark hair. "Don't worry. I won't pry into your relationship with your sisters."

Camille's stomach twisted. Her animosity was only directed at one sister.

"There's something else I need to talk to you about." His eyes seemed to plead, but then he looked away. "Please."

When he looked at her again, she saw hurt there. If only she could tell him there was nowhere she would rather be than with him. Camille couldn't stand it any longer. She walked toward him and wrapped her arms around his waist. For a second or two, he held his arms out without returning her embrace. That was okay. She understood far too well what he was going through.

He was trying to be Camille's hero—allow her to succeed, to win the contest. But Romeo could very well be the *man* of her dreams. If that was the case, why should she care about pursuing an education in art? Becoming a success. *Like Alexa.*

Why couldn't she have it both ways? The choice wasn't fair.

Finally, Romeo wrapped his arms around her and rested his chin on the top of her head. Camille sighed in contentment.

She drew in a breath and pulled away then took his hand and led him out of the kitchen, through the dining room, and out the french doors to the deck in the back. The two older women were too absorbed in the show to notice their exit.

Camille inhaled the backyard's earthy scent. Thankfully, the evenings cooled down. "I love the outdoors, don't you?" Sitting on the edge of the deck, she tugged off her shoes so she could feel the grass between her toes.

"Yes, especially from the back of a motorcycle," he said.

Camille angled her head to look at him. He was still standing, hands in his pockets. Maybe he was feeling the same as she was—the ambience was so romantic.

"About your blog. . ."

Oh boy, here it comes. Did they really need to hash through her entirely too transparent post? "So you really started reading at the beginning? I've never read anyone's blog starting from their first post."

He sat next to her and gazed into the darkness at the edge of the woods. "After our decision to step back, I guess I just wanted to know you better. I thought it would make me feel closer to you somehow."

That made her smile. "And did it?"

He nodded. "I enjoyed it very much. I think I even learned a little about Shakespeare. Now, if we ever read Shakespeare together, I'll have something to bring to the table."

Camille drew her knees up and wrapped her arms around

them. A coyote yipped in the distance. "I hear a *but* in there."

"There's a million more things I could say about your writing and your insights, but let me get to the point." He paused as if gathering his thoughts. "Camille, have you ever had anyone harass you?"

Her left foot shot off the edge, and she almost lost her balance. Romeo reached out and grabbed her shoulder to steady her. "Careful."

"Sorry. You just. . .surprised me. What are you talking about?" Problem was, Camille knew exactly what he was referring to.

"I read all the comments, or some of them anyway. Everyone seems to love the discussion. But there is this one person—I get the feeling it's a man, but who really knows? I can't understand exactly what he means, but it sounds like he. . . admires you and has been watching you."

Camille sighed. "It's not against the law, Romeo. Seriously."

"That day I came to find you in the redwoods? It was the same day he posted one of his comments. Was that why you seemed upset when I first found you?"

She hung her head. She did not want to talk about this. "What are you asking me to do? Shut down my blog? Hide from life?"

"Who was the guy at the coffee shop today? You never told me."

"Matt? Oh, just a student in my art classes. He's harmless."

Romeo crossed his arms. "How do you know?"

"I just know, okay? I've known him for several years now."

A commotion inside the house drew her attention. The sound of Alexa's voice—her older sister—drifted outside.

Her sisters had arrived a day early—no surprise there. Camille couldn't help her frown, but she'd have to hide it behind a smile before going into the house. She tugged her shoes on and hopped to her feet. She loved her sisters dearly, but Camille and Alexa never seemed to get along. Alexa was everything Camille was not, but wanted to be.

She tucked her hair back into the pins and smiled at Romeo. Poor guy. He had no idea what he was in for. "My sisters are here."

&

Romeo stood on the deck, staring at the dark woods beyond the yard, listening to the coyotes. He recalled the day he told Camille about the IED explosion and how he'd broken off his engagement to Maria. He almost wished he'd kept all that to himself. He felt vulnerable, exposed. Why had he shared so much of himself with her, and so soon?

Behind him, the sound of women excitedly giggling and chattering floated out to him. Camille spoke, but he couldn't make out the words. What was going on between her and her sisters? Whatever it was, he suspected she had many scars herself—the kind that didn't show on the outside.

The breeze picked up, rustling the leaves in the trees. He squeezed his eyes shut and imagined her face in the darkness the night he first kissed her. The moonlight allowed him to see just enough, but all the same, he knew—he could feel it across the room—she longed for him to kiss her.

Camille. . .

He was in love with this crazy, stubborn woman. Breaking off his engagement had almost been easy compared to dealing with Camille. Maria had left his side and never returned. After that, day after day, he'd been able to push her from his mind and focus on recovering. Focus on how he would face himself in the mirror every day for the rest of his life. How he would shield himself from the pain every time someone looked at him.

Yes, that had been much easier than trying to control his feelings about Camille. Part of him wanted to leave and head to Kent's place—freeing himself from that whole elfin forest magic thing she had going on.

Had she even considered how difficult it would be to leave

a place like this that was so full of beauty and wonder? And the redwoods—they were like nothing else on earth.

That art school in Chicago would be like living on a different planet for Camille. Had she thought of that? But he wouldn't try to persuade her to stay if she decided to go. Even if he did, she wouldn't listen.

She refused to listen to him on what could amount to a blog stalker—he'd done a little research on that. But she was right. There wasn't anything they could do—not really. Still, Camille needed to stay alert to her surroundings.

When she went inside to greet her sisters, he'd stayed behind on the deck. He didn't feel like being put on display. How much influence did her sisters have on her? Would they shatter the small—maybe flimsy—hope of a future with Camille?

In just a few days—a judge's decision away—he would know what course his life would take.

He took in a deep breath of cool night air and stretched. Tonight would be a good night for a ride on his motorcycle. If only he could figure out how to sneak past the women and grab his gear.

A door creaked open behind him. He didn't turn.

"Romeo, aren't you coming in?" It was Mama.

"I don't think so."

Her footfalls were slow as she made her way to him. Her hand rested on his arm. "Camille's sisters are here. Don't you want to meet them?"

He smiled down at his mother. "I'm sure I will at some point."

"They're not staying in the house tonight but at a hotel. You'll look rude if you don't come inside. Do you want to embarrass me?"

Ah, now she'd gotten to the heart of the matter.

"Mama, it's *my* appearance I'm worried about."

nineteen

Camille stood on the curb of Main Street with her sisters, Alexa and Sela, watching the bagpipe band march by. Opening day of the Redwoods Art Festival always began with a parade. Unfortunately, Camille could never listen to bagpipe music without a few chords in her heart being plucked, and tears flooded her eyes. What was it about the music of old that stirred her?

When the band moved on, a group of Asian dancers took their place, performing amazing and exotic dance moves as they waltzed forward, their music taking the place of the melodious bagpipes.

Alexa leaned in to speak in Camille's ear. "Hey, when do I get to meet Romeo?"

She shook her head. "I have no idea. Why ask me?"

The crowd clapped at a particularly amazing flip, as did Camille. Romeo had not joined them last night for introductions but instead left on his motorcycle. Camille wasn't sure how he bypassed the group to retrieve his helmet and leather. She had hoped he would escort her to the festival, but that was before her sisters had invited themselves. Now she wasn't sure what she wanted. What would Alexa's opinion of Romeo be? Camille hated that she even cared.

The dancers moved on, followed by a truck pulling a trailer of redwood carvings. The artist was one of many on exhibit hoping to sell their work. No one wanted to be a literal starving artist.

In her peripheral vision, Camille could see Alexa's stare. Camille pressed her lips together, not wanting to be drawn into a discussion about Romeo. Finally the power of her sister's

stare overcame her, and she acquiesced to the pressure—
something she'd done all too many times in her life.

Camille looked at Alexa. "What?"

"Aunt Erin told me he was injured in Afghanistan."
Alexa must be intrigued—the pupils in her bright blue eyes
dilated. Her long, brown hair hung in shiny waves across her
shoulders, lifting slightly in the breeze. Alexa was a goddess.

Yeah, a goddess sent to make my life miserable.

"But she said he used to be a very handsome man," Alexa
said, angling to find out more.

Dread wrapped around Camille's throat.

What if Alexa took an interest in him, even wanting to
film his story? After all, that was what she did—filmed
documentaries. She was always searching for a story.

Would Romeo become a curiosity to her? Or was it
something more—would Alexa become interested in him
romantically and steal him from Camille, though Camille
didn't even have him yet? Alexa was not only beautiful,
she was successful in her chosen form of art. She radiated
confidence, and men found her beauty intoxicating. She was
everything Camille was not.

Alexa could have anyone she wanted. Anyone.

The stranglehold of dread tightened around Camille's
throat until something exploded inside. "And he is *still* a very
handsome man."

She wanted to defend Romeo, but why did she say that?
Now Alexa was sure to notice just how good-looking he was.

A mischievous grin spread over Alexa's face, and her eyes
danced with glee. "You like him, don't you?" She elbowed
Sela next to her, intently watching the parade.

Sela, also a beauty with her long auburn hair, pulled her
attention from a man dressed like a lumberjack walking with
the Paul Bunyan float. He was smiling directly at her.

"What is it?" Sela was a quieter soul, especially since losing
her husband two years ago in a drowning accident.

Alexa motioned for them to follow her. Sela trailed along, but Camille stayed where she was and watched the parade. A few seconds later, Alexa grabbed her arm with an iron grip and yanked her along.

She felt like a child all over again—like she always did around Alexa. "I wanted to see the parade," she said. Oh great. Now she even sounded like a child.

Alexa stopped at the corner of a brick building, away from the crowd lining the street. Others wandered between the shops and the parade-watching throng.

When the three stood in a small circle, Alexa shoved her hair over her shoulders, still grinning in delight. "Sela, Camille likes Romeo."

Sela lost the faraway look in her eyes and focused on Camille. "That's wonderful, Camille. What's he like?"

"I never said I liked him. Alexa is imagining things." Camille started walking. A few blocks down they could avoid the parade and head to the field, where tents were set up to display local artists and booths of every kind.

Alexa strode next to her, and Sela followed. "You didn't have to say anything. I saw it in your eyes. You're an artist. You should know it's all in the eyes."

While Camille might succeed in hiding the truth from Alexa for the moment, once her sister saw the painting. . .she would *know*.

Would Romeo? He hadn't seen it yet. For some reason, she feared his response to the painting and hoped he'd keep his thoughts to himself if surrounded by people when he saw it.

"You might not want to admit it, but Aunt Erin tells me your painting for the contest is of Romeo himself. I bet anyone with a brain can look at it and tell you're in love with him."

Camille whirled on Alexa. "Are you insane? Why would I want to share my private feelings with anyone, especially you?" She couldn't believe her venomous words and cupped her mouth. "Oh Alexa. . .I'm so sorry."

Her sister's eyes widened. "Oh, that's just riveting, Camille. All I've ever tried to do is help you become successful. Encourage you. Give you direction. And this is how you thank me?"

Alexa stalked off. Sela squeezed Camille's shoulder. "Don't worry, Camille. I'll talk to her. You two really need to settle the animosity between you, though. Life is too short to hold grudges, you know?"

Sela spoke from personal experience. Camille nodded, unable to respond.

After Sela left, Camille meandered through the tents looking at the displays, her eyes unseeing, her thoughts filled with her outburst and Alexa's response.

What words of encouragement? Alexa always had to one-up Camille, show her who was best. Growing up, whatever Camille tried to do, Alexa would jump into the mix and make sure she outshone Camille.

She was left believing she could never be as good as Alexa.

Camille wasn't even beautiful. Tears streaming down her cheeks, she walked to the edge of the artist camp and wiped her eyes. Ahead of her, redwoods reached hundreds of feet into the sky, as though they wanted to touch the face of God.

Something Camille could never do unless she learned to forgive.

Oh God, what am I going to do? I had no idea this was inside of me.

And why had her animosity toward Alexa boiled to the top now, during the art festival? She should be giddy with excitement, with hope for her future.

But was it a future she wanted for herself? Or was she simply driven by her desire to be successful like Alexa? She released a breath, feeling a little better, the bitterness dissipating.

Okay, Lord, I get it now. I've pent up a lot of resentment toward my sister. But now I'm not sure if the direction I've chosen for my life is borne from bitterness. Please, just take that away from me. Let me see clearly.

Camille studied the beautiful redwoods that skirted the town and the tents—could she really leave them?—and turned back, hoping to find Alexa and apologize.

Romeo stood a few yards behind her, staring off in the distance, hands in his pockets, wearing the red baseball cap. Camille startled then smiled in delight. He usually tried to avoid crowds.

Finally, he met her gaze. The grin she loved appeared as he made his way to her. "You looked like you were having. . .a moment. So, I gave you one."

How did he know her so well?

&

Camille's eyes glistened with residual moisture, and her cheeks were still a little wet. Romeo should ask her why she'd been crying, but that might bring the tears back. He settled on a safer approach. "I thought you were here with your sisters."

She grinned up at him then looked away, biting her lip. "I was."

When she looked back at him, he thought she was going to cry again, but she didn't. Instead, she chuckled. "I wanted you to meet them, but I might have run them off."

Why would she do that?

Camille started off, heading back into the stream of people touring the tents. Romeo walked next to her.

Thinking about Camille's needs helped him to ignore the stares and glances, the children pointing and asking their parents what had happened to the man. Yes, focusing on someone else did wonders. He was here in the crowd, wasn't he?

"What happened?" he asked.

"You know what? I'm not exactly sure myself." She stopped and gazed at one of the tented booths. "Oh, look."

Romeo followed her into the tent, where she lifted a small

flowerpot with a feathery seedling.

"These are little redwood trees. Just babies." She smiled up at him. "If you end up leaving, you might take one of these little guys with you to remember me by." Her eyes dimmed, but she didn't wait for his reply. She turned her attention to the man selling the trees. "How hard are these to grow?"

The vendor dove right into a long explanation—it sounded somewhat complicated, but he talked around any issues. While he rattled on, Romeo crossed his arms and gazed out the tent opening.

You mean, if you leave.

Before he found her, he'd already walked much of the festival, hoping to see her painting. But the contest entries wouldn't be set up until later.

"You ready?" she asked, holding up the potted redwood tree.

"You bought it?" The thing looked pathetic. It wouldn't survive a day.

"Yes," she asked, running her fingers over the little green sprig. The warmth in her eyes made him doubt all over again that she could leave this place, even if she won.

He lifted his arm to escort her. "Let's go."

They walked through the field of tents, browsing various artists' wares. Romeo loved how he felt with Camille. And after spending time in Redbrook, he realized it had grown on him. The art festival just about sealed the deal for him. He would love to get serious about opening his own restaurant, or purchasing Bernardino's if he wasn't too late. But it scared him how much Mama had pinned her hopes on him staying in town and opening a restaurant. What if he failed?

Camille stooped to pet a well-groomed schnauzer on a leash, chatting and giggling with the dog's little boy. Her earlier sadness had washed away. When she smiled at Romeo, his heart nearly slid into the Pacific Ocean.

She was another woman he cared about deeply whose

hopes were pinned on something else. If she won her scholarship, she would soon be heading to school. As they strolled along, arm in arm, Romeo wasn't sure why she believed she needed the education—her paintings were exceptional—but then again, he wasn't the expert.

He could hardly stand to see her go. But they had not committed to one another because of their uncertain futures.

Were they both fools?

"So this is your Romeo?" A strong feminine voice spoke from behind.

Romeo whipped his head around to see Camille standing between two women—one with long, dark hair and the other with straight auburn hair.

"I'm Alexa," the woman with brown hair said, thrusting her hand forward. She stared into Romeo's eyes. He could tell she was a bold, strong-willed creature, willing her eyes to avoid his scar.

He took her hand. "Romeo. It's nice to meet you."

He fought the urge to tug his cap lower. *Focus on Camille.*

"And this is Sela," Camille said, squeezing the redhead's shoulder.

Romeo nodded.

"Camille hasn't told us much about you," Alexa said.

"Oh?" Romeo studied Camille. She appeared fragile between the two, but trying to hold her own. Was there a reason Camille hadn't told her sisters about him? He ignored the hurt Alexa's words could cause him. Had that been intentional? Then his gaze left Camille and traveled to Alexa and her intensely blue eyes.

She was tall for a woman and intimidating. She probably knew she was beautiful and liked to use it to her advantage. But he wasn't a psychologist.

At the awkward silence, Alexa glanced at her watch. "I say we break for lunch. Grab some food from one of these vendors and hit the beach. I need a change of scenery, don't you?" She glanced at Sela as though wanting her support.

Romeo doubted she did that often, and when he looked at Camille again, she seemed to shrivel—his little sprite, cowering beneath an overlord.

"What about you, Camille?" he asked. "Do you want to go to the beach?"

Her eyes widened as though grateful he cared about her opinion. "Sure."

They fell in stride toward the closest vendor, the menu featuring cheeseburgers, chili cheese dogs, nachos, fries, and funnel cakes. The aroma made his stomach growl, but he knew he'd pay later for eating all that grease.

Standing in line, Alexa positioned herself next to Romeo. "So have you seen your portrait?" She was tall enough to look him directly in the eyes.

He frowned. "No, I haven't. Camille wanted me to see it at the exhibit."

The woman scrutinized him but never once looked at his scar. He almost dreaded what might happen once she did.

"That's too bad," she said.

"Why do you say that?" He could tell she was manipulating him, but he'd fallen into her snare.

She shook her head as though amazed. "It's. . .incredible. That's all I can say."

"You've seen it?"

Camille jockeyed her way in the line to stand in front of Alexa. "How did you see it? You only just arrived last night."

"I have connections. That's where Sela and I went after our little quarrel. A friend took us back to see where it was stored in the exhibit hall. I tried to put in a good word for you."

"How dare you." Camille glared at Alexa. "What gives you the right to interfere?"

So his little sprite had found the strength to face her oppressor. He wished he understood more about their relationship.

"Give it a rest, will you, Camille?" Alexa loomed over her but looked at Romeo as she spoke in softer tones. "I think this could be it. You're getting that scholarship."

twenty

Late that night, Camille tossed and turned. Finally she rolled over and looked at her clock. Two thirty in the morning.

She yanked off the covers and tugged on a sweatshirt over her T-shirt. She climbed the stairs to her attic office, flipped on the small light on her desk, and curled up in the soft chair in the corner. Her little office was a place she'd grown to love and be proud of over these past two years. The room was dark save for the desk light, but Camille could still see her art supplies on the right side. Materials for her purses, along with a few of the completed bags, spread out on the floor on the other side of the room. She hadn't finished those extra bags for Mary yet.

She pressed her face into her hands. Alexa would be leaving tomorrow. Camille wasn't sure how she felt about that. She loved her sisters and, at times, wished they lived closer and could all have coffee together once in a while. But most days Camille simply felt like Alexa bulldozed right over her. Sela wasn't a concern that way.

At the beach and then back at the art festival, Alexa had pretty much made sure everyone paid attention to her—as she always did—to the exclusion of everyone else. Alexa was like a whirlwind whipping through the lives of everyone around her, leaving Camille completely drained when she finally left. Drained and frustrated. Camille wasn't sure what happened to her resolve to forgive, but considering that Alexa had committed no glaring sin, no crime against her, maybe it was Camille who needed to change.

She drew her knees up and wrapped her arms around them, resting her chin. Was Camille ungrateful? If anything, Alexa believed in her—she was so confident that Camille would win the scholarship. Camille trembled with excitement. Yet, could she believe Alexa? Her sister had always been so manipulative. Camille shouldn't listen to her regarding the scholarship, or anything else for that matter.

The house creaked—a sound only audible in the quiet of night. Romeo's photograph stared back at her from the desk. Camille rose from the chair just enough to slide it over. She settled back in and stared at the picture. It seemed her future was never in her own hands, but always riding in the hands of others. Her future was in the hands of judges right now.

She allowed herself to soak in Romeo's image. "Oh Romeo," she whispered to herself. *I don't want to leave you.*

The door rasped open. Camille froze, remembering that day weeks ago when an intruder had destroyed her painting.

Alexa poked her head in.

Camille tensed. At the moment, she would rather see the intruder.

"Camille?" Alexa whispered, stepping farther into the room.

"I couldn't sleep," Camille said.

Alexa crept over to her and sank to the floor in her soft cotton robe, lace from a silky nightie peeking out at the collar. "I couldn't sleep either."

What do you want? Hands still wrapped around her knees, Camille pressed her mouth shut.

Alexa had pulled her knees up, a mirror image of Camille on the floor. "I went to your room and knocked, then I discovered you weren't there. This was my next stop."

"Is there something on your mind?"

"You could say that." Alexa sighed. "When I decided to come see you this week, I had planned something much different from the way things turned out. We always slip into this battle. I can't really define it. But that's not what I wanted for us this time. I came to find you tonight to say how sorry I am."

Tears twisted in Camille's throat. She didn't know what to say.

"You're my sister. I love you. Maybe that's why I've tried so hard over the years to help you—but today, when I saw you with your Romeo—"

"He's not my Romeo." Camille immediately regretted her indignant tone.

"Isn't he?" Alexa weaved her fingers through her hair, pulling it back to twist into a knot behind her head. "Camille, there's no point in denying how you both feel about each other. Please, let me finish."

Camille crossed her arms and waited for the usual lecture.

Alexa clasped her hands in front of her and sighed. "Seeing you with Romeo was like seeing who you are for the first time. I don't think it's any secret that I'm a driven person." She smirked. "And. . .I've been driving you, too. But you're not like me. You saw past Romeo's scar to who he is on the inside. To be honest? I think I must be shallow. I would never be able to get past that scar."

I know.

Alexa sniffled, wiped her nose, then chuckled. "For the first time, I want to be more like you instead of the other way around. Isn't that ironic? All this time I've been trying to fix you."

Oh, is that what she calls it? Camille clenched her teeth so tightly her jaw began to ache. "So is that what you wanted to tell me—that you could never see yourself with Romeo? Are you trying to tell me that I should steer clear of him?"

"Far from it. Aren't you listening?" Alexa sat straighter. "I know that you're going to get a scholarship to the Art Institute of Chicago, just like you wanted. And that will open up a world of opportunities for you, sending you to LA or New York, places where your work will be in great demand. Or. . ."

Camille unfolded herself from the chair and sat on the edge. "Or?"

"Or, I think you and your Romeo could have a future together. Is it possible that you could have both? Maybe, but not likely. Those things rarely work out."

The voice of experience...

"You're not doing much talking here, Camille." Alexa pressed her palms in the rug behind her and leaned back, her tone composed. "I have no idea what you're thinking."

Camille took a deep breath. Alexa was trying to apologize, to understand Camille's point of view. "What I'm thinking is that before you walked into my office tonight, I decided to stop listening to you."

An awkward silence settled in the room.

Alexa arched a brow. "Riveting, Camille. But odd as it might sound, I think you and I are thinking alike for once. I've decided to stop trying to persuade you to do things to improve your quality of life, to be successful."

"Everyone has a different definition of the word *success.*" Camille squeezed her eyes shut, unsure what to think, because she was completely thrown off by this new side to Alexa. "Right now, I'm not sure what that is for me."

"And you're no longer going to hear my definition." Alexa pushed herself up from the floor. "I love you. I don't want there to be bad feelings between us." Her voice softened, and she looked—for once—almost vulnerable. "Can we start over now?"

What else could Camille do? She unraveled her arms and legs and stood to embrace Alexa. "I love you too, sis. I'm sorry for being difficult today."

Could this really be a new beginning for them? Camille gave one last hard squeeze then released Alexa.

Her sister stretched her arms out and yawned. "Now that I got that off my chest, I can sleep now." She walked to the door then turned back, hand on the knob. "I wish I could be here to see you win, but you'll call me, right? And remember, no matter what you decide in the end, I'm your biggest fan."

Alexa slipped out the door.

Camille rubbed her face, feeling more confused than ever. Hadn't she resolved never to listen to her sister?

And then she'd had the nerve to give Camille advice about Romeo.

>2

"Camille will get that scholarship, I have no doubt."

Alexa's words pounded in Romeo's head and wouldn't let go as he sped along the coastal highway on his motorcycle. No matter the outcome, one thing was certain—Camille was on the road to a future without him, a very lucrative and successful future. How could he compete with that?

She'd ridden with her sisters to the airport this morning, missing church to drop Alexa off for her flight. Sela planned to have lunch with Camille then deliver her home before driving home herself, somewhere an hour or more from here. At least that's what Mama had told him. He would be glad to have Camille to himself again, especially since they didn't have much time left.

He pulled to the side of the road, waited until a few cars passed, then made a U-turn. Camille's painting of him would finally be put on display today—and he had every intention of viewing it.

He'd gone along with her insistence that he wait to see it. He'd allowed her to have her way on that. Was he just a sucker for a pretty face, or a woman who appeared to be interested in him, despite his appearance?

When Romeo neared the outskirts of Redbrook, the traffic picked up—busier because of the art festival—and he slowed his ride, straddling his bike, feet on the ground at times when the line of cars came to a complete standstill.

The crowds were much bigger today. He hated parking his bike in the makeshift parking lot of a field, but he had no choice. Seeing the painting had become more than a mild curiosity. Now it was an obsession that drove him forward. He secured his bike and slid his dark sunglasses in place.

Romeo paid no attention to the art or the aroma of food taunting his empty stomach. Funny how one moment in time could change everything. Like the moment when he first met Camille, and she'd recharged his soul. Like yesterday when her sisters had joined them, and Camille had changed into a nervous songbird on the brink of fluttering away. And Alexa's words to him had seemed to be some sort of code for, *Don't mess up my sister's life.*

His heart was already pounding when he stepped into the hotel where the contest exhibits were displayed. He moved to slide his sunglasses off then stopped. Better to hide behind them, to hide his reaction.

As he walked through the lobby, his need to see the painting ramped up to terror. Had he made himself vulnerable by opening his heart to Camille, dropping his armor?

He hated feeling exposed like this—not only was his scar visible, but his heart felt like it was laid out for everyone to trample.

Lord, help me with this. I'm scared I'm going to see answers in that painting. Answers that I'm not going to like. . .

He jammed his hands into the pockets of his black leather jacket and moved to the side, trying to blend with others viewing the various paintings on the wall—watercolors, pastels, oils. The room was a maze of artwork—Romeo's portrait could be anywhere.

Easy now, breathe.

A large canvas—about six by four—took up one section of the wall. A huge red splotch ran diagonally along the painting, covering black streaks. He listened to a woman in her midforties explain to someone—maybe her son?—what she saw in this particular painting. Romeo wished Camille had chosen to paint something abstract like that—completely nebulous.

Harmless.

A person could construe any meaning they wanted. From

the sound of it, the woman had issues with her ex-husband.

Romeo stepped to the next painting to study the patterns. He could be at this all day, studying works of art until he gained control over his nerves. He had to approach Camille's painting completely calm and in command of his emotions.

Now that he'd stepped away from her world for a moment, he saw her painting for what it was—a threat. Looking at himself in that portrait could very well destroy him.

But he had to see. Seeing it would be like facing himself— only without the scar. Still, he believed he had to face the truth. Whatever it was.

And no matter the outcome.

Across the room a few people stood in front of a painting. Some of them moved on to the next, but as soon as they were out of his line of vision. . .he saw it.

His racing heart slowed.

He stopped breathing.

When his lungs began to scream, Romeo drew in the smallest of breaths. He wasn't ready. Hadn't expected to see it yet.

He took one step forward, then another. Each step got easier until, finally, he strode diagonally across the floor space between the exhibits to the far side of the hall. In a corner with a flickering light, Camille's painting of Romeo hung on the wall.

He found himself standing all alone to observe his portrait. . . .

A portrait of him. . .*with* his scar.

This entire time he was expecting to view himself as he once was—unflawed, handsome.

Despite the scar, the man in the portrait *was* handsome. This man couldn't be Romeo.

More emotion, more passion than ever lived inside Romeo radiated from this man's eyes, as if the painting were alive. The artist left no doubt that the man in the painting was a hero. His face said everything that words could not—he was sacrifice and obedience wrapped into one person.

Alexa's words about Camille getting the scholarship resonated through his mind again, and now he understood her confidence. His heart lay gaping, and the past came crashing back. The tour in Afghanistan. Alpha Company. On patrol in the Zhari district. The roadside bomb exploding. Tears flooding Maria's eyes when Romeo told her he couldn't marry her.

He'd hurt her deeply. And hurt himself, beyond the physical wound. The pain washed over him again now.

And all because of that scar.

He stared at it now. How had Camille painted everything in such detail? He'd only wanted to see himself as he once was. He hadn't realized that until this moment.

Grown men weren't supposed to cry, but his eyes were stinging.

At least he'd kept on his sunglasses. *Thank You, God.*

When he gained control, he slid them to the top of his head so he could study the details more clearly.

Maria never saw him when he was whole the way Camille saw him scarred. She'd portrayed all that she saw of him in the portrait, *with* his scar. He wasn't sure how, but he could feel her love for him in the painting.

A gasp resounded to his right. "The painting is of you, isn't it?" a woman asked.

Romeo didn't answer. He put the sunglasses back in place and headed straight for the door. A million confusing thoughts and questions flooded his mind and heart.

At the door, he glanced back to the painting one more time.

Camille's student, Matt, stood in front of it, staring.

twenty-one

After lunch with Sela, Camille had spent the rest of the day working on additional bags for Mary like she'd promised. She wished her hands weren't shaking. Just thinking about her painting set her nerves on edge. The art would be on display for the rest of the ten-day festival, along with various activities and events. She would go see it in good time.

When Sela had dropped her off at home, Romeo's motorcycle was gone. At first Camille had been glad he wasn't around. Alexa's apology and change of heart last night had given Camille more than enough to think about. Facing Romeo right now would be too hard. So much time wasted on dreaming and hoping, and now she was no longer certain the dream was even hers. And if not, she'd spent far too much of her life competing with Alexa.

She lay down on the rug and stared at the ceiling. Where did all this uncertainty leave her? Aunt Erin expected her to move on, and she could hear her voice now, scolding Camille for throwing her future away for a man.

Stella wanted her gone, for her son's sake. And Romeo? He'd not made any commitments to her. Not even told her that he loved her. Camille would be a fool to toss her plans aside because she cared for him, wouldn't she? In that, she supposed she had to agree with Aunt Erin.

She closed her eyes and sighed. Her life would have been completely different if Dad hadn't left. Her mother had been a terrific single mom, but since she died, Camille had nowhere to turn for motherly advice.

What would you say about Romeo, Mom?
Where was he today anyway?

Camille hadn't slept last night, and the strong urge to nap overwhelmed her. She stretched out on the floor, planning to close her eyes for a few minutes. When she woke up, her mouth hung open. She sensed that she wasn't alone. Camille opened her eyes.

Dark eyes set in a rugged, unforgettable face stared down at her.

"Romeo," she said and smiled. Her heart fluttered, and she wondered if she had been drooling. "What are you doing here?"

"Watching you take a nap." He grinned down at her. "I didn't know that Sleeping Beauty snored." He offered his hand.

"You, sir, are incorrigible." She laughed and thrust her hand into his, allowing him to assist her to her feet. Despite all her confusing thoughts, she was happy beyond words to see him. She smoothed out her wild hair. "Where have you been all day?"

"Working on a project." He took both her hands in his. "There's something I want to do."

"Okay."

The playful grin remained in place, and something new danced in his eyes. He led her out of the attic, holding her hand.

She followed him down the stairs, a nervous laugh bubbling up. "I don't understand. What are we doing?"

"You'll see." He glanced at her then took care to maneuver the staircase.

At the bottom, he held a finger to his lips. Stella and Aunt Erin clattered around in the kitchen, making dinner. Romeo led Camille into the small den off the living room.

Romeo again took both Camille's hands in his.

The enchantment behind his eyes made her heart dance. "You're kind of scaring me, but in a good way. What's going on?"

He laughed. "Sorry for the drama. I want to do something

with you before it's too late. We keep saying we're going to read Shakespeare, and we never do. Will you give me that tonight, Camille? Before it's too late."

Before it's too late? Sadness flitted across her heart. She shook her head, wondering at his crazy antics. "Sure, all you have to do is ask."

"And that's what I'm doing."

Camille didn't know what to make of this. Surely he had something more up his sleeve. "All right, I'll play along."

She loved the smile he gave her.

Camille took the script he offered and settled on the sofa. *Romeo and Juliet.* Why that one? She looked up at Romeo, who'd taken the chair catty-corner to hers, and found him gazing at her expectantly.

"Where did you get this?" She chuckled. "It's not one of mine."

"Just read. I want to understand it."

"You realize this is a tragedy, right? It doesn't end well."

"We'll see."

Indeed. She cleared her throat and began. Camille easily fell into the rhythm that was Shakespeare, fancying herself a Shakespearean actor. Romeo had known he would make her happy with this. And she was.

After the first scene, she glanced at him. "Did you understand any of that?"

He simply smiled. "Read on. When the play is done, you can explain it to me."

Camille continued reading another scene, and then another, falling into the passion and emotions that she loved about this playwright, that so many loved about him. She would have plenty to blog about. At one point, tears welled in her eyes. She hated reading out loud with Romeo hearing the tremor in her voice. She would make him read the next act.

Finally, in the fifth scene, Romeo sees Juliet for the first time. He knows he'd never been in love until then, and they share their first kiss. Camille desperately wanted to watch how the scene affected Romeo. She dared to look away from the script and, at the warmth in Romeo's eyes, heat raced up her neck.

"That's enough." He stood. "I think I could understand this better if we act it out."

Needing to expand her lungs for air, Camille stood as well. "You want to act out that entire scene?"

Romeo took a step toward her and then another. "No, not the entire scene." He swept her up in his arms and pressed his lips against hers, gently at first, then more intensely.

He released her, leaving her breathless.

"Romeo. . ." She touched her cheeks, feeling the heat there, and slowly lifted her gaze to his.

Now she understood the glimmer in his eyes.

"You had me read Shakespeare just so you could kiss me?"

He ran his thumb down her cheek. "You didn't like it?"

Be still, my heart. "I see we've tossed taking things slowly to the wind."

"I spent this afternoon at the Shakespearean theater in Clearing, and that's what they performed. I simply had to try that." He smiled, clearly pleased with himself. "I'm glad I did."

Camille's heart skipped then waltzed. "I'm glad you did, too."

His smile leveled. "I went to the exhibit today."

Her heart missed a beat.

He saw the portrait.

twenty-two

Camille stepped from his arms. Barely breathing, she watched him, waiting for him to say more. He stared at her, equally intense, and she sensed he wanted her to respond first.

Finally, when she could no longer stand the force of his gaze, she whispered, "And?"

She supposed if he were angry, he wouldn't be standing here now, kissing her. He wouldn't have listened to Shakespeare just so he could kiss her in a surprising and romantic way. There was so much about this man that she loved.

She'd wanted to be with him at the exhibit when he saw the fruit of her labor. And yet she'd dreaded it at the same time.

What had she expected? For him to simply wait for her?

The corner of his mouth curved. He shook his head slightly, as though searching for the right words. "You don't need to worry about the competition."

She sucked in a breath. "Really?"

Delight and something distant and unreadable wavered behind his eyes.

"Wait. You're not just saying that?"

"No, I'm not just saying that." His voice was gruff, choked with emotion.

What did he think about her winning? Was he glad for her or distraught at the idea that she would soon be leaving? And if he believed she would leave, why this little drama tonight and the kiss? Why remove the speed bumps they'd put in place to slow the romance?

His response, though flattering—she should be ecstatic

and infused with hope for the future—left her deflated and empty. Was that it? She needed to know how the painting affected him personally. "What else?"

Romeo's smile faltered.

You don't like it. I thought I'd captured you in the painting. She couldn't look at him anymore and stared at the script still in her hand instead. Disappointment infused her—she'd wanted so much more from his reaction. She wanted to hear the words from him. Maybe if she pressed him, he would tell her what she needed to know.

She swallowed, still not looking at him. "What did it make you feel when you first saw it? What was your first impression?"

"There you are, kids." Aunt Erin scurried into the room with two plates of pie. Behind her, Stella carried a tray with a teapot and cups. "We thought we'd eat our apple pie in here. Won't you join us?"

"I'd love some pie, thank you," Romeo replied.

Already on the verge of tears, Camille was in no mood for Stella's plan to thwart their relationship. She was surprised Romeo took the women's interruption so patiently.

"Thanks, but I'm not hungry. I think I'll go up to my room," she said, turning to leave.

Romeo grabbed her arm and leaned closer, whispering in her ear, "Please. . .stay."

The way he spoke the words, she was candy in his hands and could melt right there. She forced a smile. "I'll have some tea then."

Camille took the cup that Stella offered. When Romeo patted the cushion next to him, she sat, glad she'd stayed.

Stella set her pie plate in her lap, her face creased with a familiar look of consternation. "So, when should you hear the news?"

The question was meant to remind Camille that she shouldn't toy with Romeo's feelings, no doubt. "In two days we should know."

Aunt Erin returned with another plate of pie for herself. "Are you excited or nervous?"

"A little of both, I think." Camille laughed, uncomfortable with all the attention, especially because she shared the love seat with Romeo.

He slid his hand over hers and squeezed. The next thing she knew, they were holding hands. Just like that. In front of his mother. *Romeo, what are you doing?* If he wanted to be a good son, then why was he defying Stella's wishes?

Camille suppressed a grin.

"And then you'll be off to Timbuktu, won't you?" Stella glared at Camille over the rim of her cup.

"I'll cross that bridge when I get to it." Camille tipped the last of the tea into her mouth. She stared into her empty cup and squeezed Romeo's hand. Her confusion began to clear. Attending a premiere art university wasn't going to make her happy like she thought. No longer did the idea of becoming a big success, of having a future in a big city that would put her talents to use in a big way, leave her giddy with excitement.

Feeling Romeo's eyes on her, she slid her gaze to him, and he smiled.

What was happening to her?

Could her excitement and nervousness be coming from none other than Romeo?

⋅❧⋅

Later that night, Camille sat up in bed, feeling a strange, warm glow around her—she knew it had to be her love for Romeo. She opened her laptop to read her blog post again.

The events of the evening still played in her mind. First, Romeo had surprised her by asking her to read *Romeo and Juliet*, and then he'd kissed her. She knew in her heart that he loved her, but he wouldn't say so because he didn't want to keep her from her plans. Then her aunt and Stella had tried to separate them, but their interference had only forced the issue—Romeo and Camille were in a romantic relationship.

It was out in the open for everyone to see.

And to end the day, Camille had written a blog post filled with passion and meaning, as though she was seeing everything through a new light. And...she was.

She scrolled through the comments to see if others would respond to the post. Thankfully, she saw no more posts from Don John, who'd apparently gotten bored with her blog. Several of the comments were complimentary, as she'd hoped.

But another post made her heart flip. She giggled.

An anonymous poster wrote, *Tonight with you and Shakespeare was incredible. Your Romeo.*

"Oh Romeo..." *I love you.*

When, if ever, would he tell her the same?

Unsure how to set up an online chat, Camille got out of bed and found her cell. She texted him with a private response.

You, me, and Shakespeare forever. Then she deleted the message. She couldn't send that.

A light knock sounded against the door. Romeo would never come to her bedroom, so it couldn't be him. "Come in."

Aunt Erin slipped through the door and closed it. She frowned. "You look like a teenager. Are you texting someone? Let me guess. Romeo?"

Camille pressed the phone against her chest. Teenager, indeed. "You sound like Stella."

"Perhaps you should listen," she said, then tugged the chair from the desk to sit.

Dropping onto the bed, Camille felt like a little kid waiting for a lecture.

"Stella and I have known each other for years, been friends for years. And this, whatever it is between you and Romeo, is putting a strain on our friendship. Hasn't Romeo seen enough heartache to last a lifetime?" She sighed. "I just want you to be absolutely sure about what you're doing before you go and break that young man's heart."

"And what about my heart?" Camille looked down at her hands, regretting her harsh tone. Aunt Erin couldn't know that Romeo was as much to blame. He was the one pursuing Camille.

Was he trying to woo her? Convince her to stay with him and forget her plans for the future?

Camille smiled to herself, liking that idea very much.

&

Sitting in the far corner at the back of the Internet café, Romeo sipped his coffee as he did more research on restaurants, trying to come up with ideas for something new and amazing.

Camille sat across from him, her fingers tapping on the keys as she worked on her *In Love with Shakespeare* blog. Her last few posts proved that not only could she paint, she had a serious knack for writing. Her readers grew by the day. She concentrated on the screen with an air of happiness, like she wasn't all nerves as she waited to hear the contest results. She'd pinned a lot on that. More than any person should, in Romeo's opinion. But Camille wasn't just any person, any artist.

But right now, he didn't care.

Romeo wasn't sure how it happened, but it was like he and Camille had a silent agreement between them to enjoy whatever time they had left. To that end, they spent almost every moment together, neither of them talking about the future or the outcome of the contest.

Romeo had entered discussions with Bernardino about his restaurant but had put his plans on hold until he could know for sure his future—with or without Camille. He'd vowed not to stand in the way of her dream, but he had second thoughts after meeting Alexa. She had way too much influence over Camille. He was beginning to believe that Camille wouldn't be happy moving from the redwoods she loved, attending school—and for what? What could they teach her about art that she didn't already inherently know? Nor could he see her working in corporate America. But in the end, it was her decision.

She was the most sensitive woman he'd ever known. That probably played a part in her extraordinary talent. Her portrait of him attested to that. He'd never told her what he really felt about the painting. If he ever did, it would be at the right moment.

He reached across the little table in the café and placed his hand on hers. She smiled over her laptop at him, unspoken love in her eyes, then focused again on writing.

Lord, am I going to lose her?

twenty-three

Camille finished typing and published her post. Funny—she'd gone from working on her blog in the evenings after what she considered her work hours, to typing up a blog post right in the middle of the afternoon. Romeo stared at her across the table, and the heat rose in her neck and face.

The way the ideas were flooding her lately, she knew exactly the reason. Romeo inspired her for so much more than just her art—he'd brought Shakespeare alive to her.

All this time, she was reading, studying, and writing about Shakespeare so she could engage with others on the topic, but it wasn't until Romeo came into her life that she truly understood the passion of emotions Shakespeare wrote about.

Already there was a new anonymous comment. "*Parting is such sweet sorrow. . .*" *May I escort you to the exhibit tonight? Your Romeo.*

Camille let her gaze slide over to him. He had that roguish grin on again. "You are a flirt, you know that?" she teased.

"Today is the day, Camille." His grin wavered. "I want to be there with you when they make the announcement."

She trembled at the thought. "I'm not sure, but maybe they will contact the winners before they announce them tonight." She had tried to tell herself she didn't care about getting a degree or being a success. And if Romeo hadn't come into her life, she would never have thought twice about her dream. Winning would be more than her ticket to success—it would mean validation for her efforts as an artist.

"Either way, I want to be with you."

"I need to go home and change." Camille closed her laptop

and glanced down at her tie-dyed T-shirt and capris. "I'm not exactly presentable."

Something behind her drew Romeo's gaze away. His expression grew dark, but a smile suddenly appeared.

Matt stood at their table, looking down at them. "Have you heard anything yet?"

"You mean about the contest?" Camille shook her head. "No, and you?"

He'd entered a different category—watercolors. Still, the winner over all the categories would win the scholarship. That's why Camille had searched so hard for something that inspired her, something that would stand out.

He licked his lips then glanced around the crowded café. "Nothing. Are they supposed to call us or something?"

Camille shrugged. "I'm sure that information is available somewhere, but I plan to be there when they announce the winners."

"Well, I guess I'll see you tonight then." Matt nodded to Romeo before he left.

Romeo leaned against the seat back and crossed his arms, studying her. "He's one of your students. You know he likes you, right?"

Glancing around to make sure that Matt was out of earshot, she leaned closer. "It used to be a minor annoyance—he's always painting things for me. But like I said before, he's harmless."

Romeo scowled, looking unconvinced.

Camille scowled back. "Don't worry about him. Everything is going to change tonight. Speaking of which, I've got to go change."

Desperation fell over Romeo's face, and he reached across the table, grabbing her arm just as she made to rise. "I need to talk to you about something serious."

She laughed. She'd been with him most of the day, and now he wanted to talk serious? Still, the urgency in his face compelled her to sit back on the edge of her chair. "What is it?"

Romeo's cell rang. He glanced at the call and frowned. "Give me a minute." He answered the call.

Camille would give him five seconds because she really needed to go. She wanted to be beautiful tonight for the event—for Romeo. That was the only reason she would be in a hurry to leave his side.

When he finished, he closed his laptop. "I've been talking to Bernardino about his restaurant. I put things off with him because I wasn't sure about my future. But he says it's urgent that we meet tonight. I'm not sure how long it will take."

Bernardino's? The news startled Camille, but she brought her focus back. "Are you saying you aren't escorting me?"

Romeo lifted her hand to his lips. "I wouldn't miss that for the world."

"Is that what's so serious?" she asked.

"Only part of it. Can we talk later? I've got to go. The sooner I can meet with him, the sooner I can change and be ready for you."

She nodded as Romeo released her hand and slid away from her. He seemed to forget that Camille was leaving, too, and left her sitting at the table. The man was definitely preoccupied. He maneuvered through the growing crowd that had come to the café in search of coffee, croissants, and free Internet access.

She had the oddest sense that his walking away from her meant something, and she wasn't sure she liked it. Were they about to go on their separate paths?

❧

Almost as soon as Camille arrived home to change, she received a text from Romeo stating that he would have to meet her at the art exhibit instead of the house.

She sagged at the thought. He wouldn't have time to change into his new suit. But the fact was, he'd offered to escort her, and he was actually going to the event. She knew how hard that was for him. He'd come so far since arriving here, not nearly as self-conscious about his scar.

After Camille showered, she put on one of her fancier dresses, though it still might look like a potato sack compared to the women who arrived in satin and sequins. She spun to watch the skirt swirl, loving how she looked in the mirror. She hoped Romeo would love it, too. But why was she torturing herself with thoughts of him if they were just going to part? Why had he come into her life when he did? He wasn't making any promises. What if she won? Could she throw the opportunity away without some sort of commitment?

But what if she had a commitment? Was she ready?

Was that what Romeo wanted to talk to her about? Was he thinking along the same lines as she was?

The questions were driving her crazy. With a few minutes to spare before she needed to leave, she perused her blog and found more comments, including one from the anonymous poster who always signed, 'Your Romeo.' She smiled, wanting to be with him. His posts always filled her with delight—she loved to dance with him this way.

It read, *Meet me under the redwood tree, for a midsummer night's dream.*

Camille fell back on her bed and stared at the ceiling. She saw only Romeo's face—after all, she'd spent hours upon hours painting it. The guy was dreamy in so many unexpected ways.

Someone knocked on her door then opened it. Aunt Erin stuck her head in. "Stella and I are ready. Sure you don't want to ride with us?"

Camille sat up. "No, I've got to meet Romeo before the exhibit, then we'll go together from there."

"I thought he was meeting you there."

"No, he wants to meet at the redwood tree."

Aunt Erin frowned. "I'm not sure I like the sound of that."

Romeo must have something special planned, or else why would he ask to meet there? It was a special place to her, and he knew that.

She pressed a hand against her swirling stomach—surely he wouldn't. . .propose. Tonight of all nights. There was so much between them that they needed to work out—like their futures.

"All right then, sweetie." Aunt Erin leaned forward and kissed Camille on the forehead. "Whatever the outcome, know that I'm very proud of you."

"Thanks." Camille rubbed her temples.

"Are you going to be all right?" Aunt Erin asked.

"It's just nerves. Too much is happening all in one night."

❧

Romeo tried to blend into the brick wall of the building and become invisible as people passed him on their way inside the exhibit hall. A lot of people were arriving early. How many people would the place hold? So far, he hadn't seen any sign of Camille. She wasn't answering her cell.

The unexpected meeting with Bernardino had left his head spinning with opportunities—but then, they, too, depended on Camille.

He wished he'd opted to go home and change, but he didn't want to make Camille late. Not tonight. What if she won and wasn't there to hear the announcement or receive her award? He didn't want her to miss that moment.

There they are.

He watched Erin park her car in a nearby handicapped parking spot, due to Mama's arthritis. He breathed a little easier.

A few people glanced his way as they passed before entering the building. He wondered if they recognized him from the portrait. Despite the usual guarded looks, Romeo found himself smiling instead of drawing back into himself. Could it be that he was finally moving beyond his injury and memories of the war? If so, then he was ready for whatever happened tonight. For whatever future awaited him.

Lord, if Camille feels the same about me, please help me accept her love.

He'd come to dread that Camille would win a scholarship, that she would leave this little town—and leave him. But he'd come up with a plan.

Mama and Erin approached slowly, unhurried by others who moved much faster. He stepped from the wall.

"Mama," he said and took her arm, smiling. "Where's Camille?"

Erin stared at him with a blank look. The skin between her brows crinkled. "I thought she was with you."

"I'm supposed to meet her here."

"No, you're supposed to meet her under the redwood tree."

"What? Why would I do that?"

"I don't know, but that's what she said."

At that moment, a man wearing a suit rushed from the exhibit hall. "Excuse me, excuse me," he said as he made his way through the crowd heading indoors. He walked straight to Erin.

"I can't get ahold of your niece. Where can I find her?"

"Why, what's wrong?" Erin asked.

He leaned in to whisper, "Her painting was stolen."

"What?"

"How could this happen?"

Mama and Aunt Erin spoke together.

A fierce knot grew inside Romeo's insides. "I'll find her."

Romeo left them and jogged to his motorcycle. Now he knew why Camille didn't answer her phone. There was no reception in the redwoods. He started his motorcycle and tried to work his way between the cars. Traffic was moving way too slowly. He wished now that he had asked Erin more questions about Camille. Did she leave him a message that failed to connect to his phone?

It didn't make any sense to him—they hadn't discussed anything about meeting there earlier. Then there was the fact of her stolen painting. It had to be the same person who destroyed the other one in her house. Of that, he had no doubt.

Something heavy settled in the pit of his stomach. Romeo accelerated and pressed himself against the bike, hoping to make record time.

twenty-four

The excitement of meeting Romeo under the redwood tree dissipated somewhat as Camille made her way along the trail in her hiking boots. She'd wanted to look glamorous for him, but she'd made a wise decision in trading out her pumps for the boots. Though it was early evening and there were still a couple of hours of sunlight left, darkness would settle in the redwood forest first.

Camille chuckled—she didn't exactly fit into the stylish mold. But if she followed through with plans that would catapult her into the professional world, she'd certainly have to adjust.

Finally, she made her way off the trail to her beloved redwood. She fancied it had grown for two thousand years, waiting for the moment when Romeo would propose to her under its branches.

She was a hopeless romantic.

She sighed as she reached the grove. He wasn't there yet. She'd not seen his motorcycle in the parking lot, but maybe she'd missed it. She glanced at her watch. He'd better hurry. The awards ceremony would start soon. Not wanting to snag her dress, she leaned against the bark with her hands pressed behind her for support.

Someone stepped out from the other side of the tree. Her heart fluttered, crazy with nerves. If he proposed, what would she say?

But it was Matt who stood before her, wearing a suit and a wide grin. "I was afraid you wouldn't get my message, that you wouldn't come. You've made me very happy."

Her limbs froze. "Uh. . . Matt, what are you doing here?"

Matt took her hand in his and gently lifted and kissed it, just as Romeo had done earlier today in the café.

A chill ran up her spine, and she yanked her hand away from his. "I'm sorry, Matt, I'm just not interested in you that way."

Matt's smile faded, and he pulled a photograph from his pocket. "Is this the man you thought you were meeting here?"

Camille peered at the photograph of her painting of Romeo—the one without the scar. She gasped. So Matt was the one who broke into her house and destroyed the painting?

Anger boiled inside, quickly doused by growing fear. Her throat closed up. This guy was crazy—and dangerous.

"Why, Matt?" Camille choked out the words. "Why are you doing this?" She glanced toward the trail, wondering if she could escape.

"Because!" Matt's face turned red as he spat the word. "I have loved you for years. How could you not know? To think, all the paintings I've given you." He calmed and moved closer, running his thumb down her cheek. Then, more softly, "And you choose a man with a hideous scar over *me*?"

Tears gathered in Camille's eyes.

Astonishingly, they did in Matt's as well. "I should be the one asking why," he went on. "Why, Camille? Why have you betrayed me like this?" He gripped her wrist and squeezed.

Camille's pulse throbbed in her head, flooding her ears. She could hardly think what to say, but she knew that if she was going to survive, she had to speak very carefully.

She closed her eyes and drew in a long breath. "You're right, Matt, I've made a terrible mistake. I see that now. Romeo's scar is hideous. I could never love him."

Matt loosened his grip on her but didn't let go. She couldn't outrun him anyway.

Lord, help me! The only thing she could do was play along.

He pulled her close and wove his hands into the hair at the back of her head.

Oh no. He's going to kiss me. She clenched her fists. *Lord, help me go through with it.*

When Matt pressed his lips against hers, she tried to imagine Romeo. But hiding her revulsion was beyond difficult.

Finally, he released her and caressed her face with his fingers. "You don't have any idea how long I've wanted to kiss you. Thanks for meeting me here. I love you, Camille."

He nudged her chin up and peered into her eyes. Camille squeezed them shut, tears sliding from the corners. She knew what he wanted to hear.

But she just couldn't say the words.

ھ

Romeo stood behind a copse of redwoods, pain gripping every inch of his body. Erin had been wrong—Camille had planned to meet Matt here, not Romeo. What was going on?

He stumbled away from the scene he'd just witnessed. He could hardly believe it, and yet he'd seen it with his own eyes. Camille kissing Matt, speaking of Romeo like he was the scourge of the earth, saying that his scar was hideous to her.

Romeo wanted to fall to his knees. In his heart, he was already sobbing.

Why, God? Why did she let me believe, lead me on like this? He rushed down the trail, putting distance between him and the couple. Why had he believed she could love him? Why had he opened himself up to her?

She knew him like no one else—he'd seen that with his own eyes in her painting. But he only *thought* he knew her.

Romeo stopped abruptly, almost tripping forward. *No.* He would not allow his insecurity, his old self-loathing to twist his thoughts. With God's help, he'd grown beyond that now.

The truth stared back at him. Camille was not being genuine. He heard fear in her voice, not love. Romeo knew how love sounded coming from Camille.

In the distance, she screamed.

Romeo sprinted back to the tree, hating himself for doubting her and leaving her to be Matt's victim. "Camille!" he yelled, letting Matt know she wasn't alone.

Matt pressed Camille against the tree.

Romeo gripped the man's collar, yanking with all his force, then shoved him to the ground. Hands fisted, Romeo placed a booted foot on Matt's midsection and pressed hard, daring him to fight back.

Just one good punch to the nose. That's all I want.

Matt's face crumpled in anguish, and he scrambled away from Romeo. "You're as pathetic as she is. Go ahead. Take her if you want. She's all yours." He jumped up and ran away, glancing behind him only once.

Romeo was stunned he'd given up so easily. He watched to make sure the guy was gone then turned his attention to Camille. Tears streaked her face as she came to him and sobbed into his shoulder. He held her tightly, knowing words were not enough. When she drew in a shaky breath, her crying spent, Romeo released her.

He cupped her cheeks with his hands. "Why did you come here?"

"Because," she said, tears lacing her voice, "because I thought it was you. It was anonymous and signed, 'Your Romeo,' just like you always do." Camille lost it again.

He'd been such an idiot, making it too easy for the blog stalker to take advantage.

"Come on, let's get you out of here. It's going to start getting dark soon." He held her hand and led her from the tree. "We need to call the police, too."

"No, wait." She tugged him back.

He turned to look at her. "What is it?"

"You said you had something to talk to me about. That's why I thought you wanted to meet me at the redwood tree— the tree that I love. Can we. . . I need to have a good memory to replace what just happened."

Romeo nodded, but he was unsure if anything he had to say would erase this. "I spoke too soon when I said I needed to talk to you." He stared at the ground, ashamed. "I was afraid of losing you. I *am* afraid of losing you."

"I'm sorry if you heard the words I said to Matt, sorry if I hurt you. But you know I didn't mean them, right?" Her tears started again. "He tricked me to get here, and I think he actually made himself believe I wanted to be with him and not you. I knew then that he was crazy."

"You did what you had to do." Romeo wanted to kick himself for doubting her.

"Just tell me what you wanted to say, Romeo."

He stared at her, wanting to tell her everything he felt about her, but after what Matt had done, he felt his words would fall flat. "We should get you to the exhibit and the announcements, Camille." He hesitated, remembering.

"What is it? You know something, don't you?" Camille tugged at his shirt.

He took a deep breath. "Your painting was stolen."

Her eyes grew wide. "Are you serious?"

She covered her mouth then turned and walked a few paces from him. When she turned back she was smiling—not what he'd expected. She threw her arms out. "I don't care! I don't care. Romeo, I don't care."

He laughed along with her. "Of course you care. And it makes no difference—you probably won anyway."

"Don't you see? That's what I'm saying. I don't care if I win or not. I don't care about the scholarship." She swirled around, her skirt flying up like a movie star from the fifties.

The sight of her dizzied him. She reminded him of a fairy as always—but he'd never seen her this beautiful. She ran to him and flung her arms around him. He swung her in a circle, playing the part.

Finally, he put her on her feet and kissed her. "I was going to tell you that if you have to go away, I want to go with you.

I love you, Camille."

"Oh, Romeo. I love you, too. I thought when you said you had something to tell me, and then you wanted to meet me at the tree, I thought. . ."

"You thought what?" Did she think he would propose? Was he reading her right? "What I wanted to tell you—"

"Yes?"

"—is about the painting."

She frowned.

Before she could speak, Romeo placed a finger over her lips. "I saw myself in your painting. I don't know how you did it, Camille, but you captured me, the real me, all of me in that painting. You saw past the scar to the real me. You saw more of me than Maria did before I was injured. Or even Mama, who has known me my whole life."

"It means everything to hear you say that. But you're wrong."

Romeo didn't understand. "What are you saying?"

"I couldn't possibly capture you in a painting. It would take a lifetime spent with you before I could do that."

Romeo grinned, feeling the meaning beneath her words to his core. "Marry me?"

Her eyes glistened, joy behind them. "There's nothing I'd rather do. 'I love you with so much of my heart that none is left to protest.'"

He cocked a half grin. "That must be from Shakespeare."

"You're learning. *Much Ado about Nothing*."

"I've got one."

"Is it from Shakespeare?"

"Something better. *Ti amo, vita mia*."

Her stomach flip-flopped. "Italian." She grinned. "Oh Romeo, you're so romantic. What does it mean?"

"I love you, my life."

twenty-five

Camille stood at the kitchen sink getting a glass of filtered water, Romeo at her side. After everything that had happened over the last hour, she wasn't in the mood to fight the crowds or learn the outcome of the art contest. So they headed back to the house. Camille called Aunt Erin and Stella, and they were on their way home, too.

Besides, she had her future standing right next to her. To think she'd wasted so much thought and effort on something that wasn't what she really wanted, wasn't what God had for her after all. But she couldn't have known that without Romeo's help.

Her stomach growled. "I'm hungry. You want some leftovers? I think we still have plenty of your pasta."

Romeo wrapped his arms around her waist and pressed his forehead against hers. "You know, you never told me your secret ingredient."

Her laugh bubbled in her chest before spilling out. "Uh-uh. You're not getting that from me."

"Oh no?" He quirked a brow, ready for a challenge.

Camille slipped from his arms and moved away, stepping around the kitchen table. Laughter filled the kitchen as she stood on the opposite side of the table, dodging his attempts to catch her. By the look in his eyes, he was ready to climb over it.

She giggled. He scrambled over and caught her in his arms, laughing. Camille giggled so hard she couldn't get her breath. Romeo turned her to him and kissed her face, making his way to her mouth.

"Not until we're married," she said, laughing with pleasure.

"I have to keep that in the family."

"Then we must elope," he said, finally kissing her on the lips. "I have to know your secret ingredient."

"What. . .is going on in here?"

Stella stood in the center of the kitchen, red faced with hands on her hips. Aunt Erin shuffled in behind her and scowled.

Romeo and Camille stilled, though Camille had to work to stifle her laughter. He released her and shoved his hand through his hair. After a quick wink at Camille, he faced his mother. This could be a defining moment for their relationship—would Romeo stand up to her, tell her the truth?

Stella began a long, heated spiel in Italian.

"Mama, please, in English." Romeo held out his hands. "For Camille, for. . .my fiancée."

Smiling, he tugged Camille to him by the waist and kissed the side of her head.

Stella's mouth hung open.

Moments passed, it seemed, and Camille held her breath, waiting.

Stella's eyes filled with tears. Her face transformed from a look of shock into a huge smile that she covered with her hands, muffling more Italian words. When she dropped her hands, she moved faster than Camille had ever seen to stand before her. "Oh my daughter. You are everything I've wanted for my Romeo."

Camille stared up at Romeo's smiling eyes while Stella almost suffocated her with hugs. Aunt Erin congratulated Romeo, her eyes misting as well. Camille couldn't have asked for more in Stella's response, but she found it confusing.

Stella took a step back and dabbed at her eyes with a tissue. "After I saw your painting, I knew how much you loved my Romeo, that you were the one. And Romeo, you are such a good son. I couldn't ask for better."

"You saw the painting?" Camille asked.

"They recovered the stolen painting." Stella smiled. "Someone had stashed it behind some boxes in the back, that's all."

Aunt Erin drew in a breath. "Sounds like this has been a busy night for everyone." She disappeared into the foyer and returned, holding the portrait. After removing another picture, she hung it on a nail in the kitchen. "We have to return it for the exhibit, but I asked to bring it home for tonight. Considering what happened, they were more than willing to let me."

Everyone gathered around Romeo's portrait. Aunt Erin looked at Camille. "Aren't you curious about the winner?"

"I'm curious, yes, but it doesn't matter now," Camille said, believing her words.

"I'm sorry, sweetie, you didn't win. I think the winner was a woman in your class." Her brow furrowed as she tried to remember. "Lorraine?"

"Sweet Lorraine won the contest?" Camille squealed. "They're going to award her with the scholarship? Wow. Lorraine is going to get an art degree at eighty-seven."

"The director asked me to give you this." Aunt Erin handed Camille an envelope. Probably an apology and explanation for her stolen portrait. Was the theft a factor in the contest outcome? Camille opened the envelope and tugged out an official letter.

"Oh my. . ." Camille stumbled over to a kitchen chair and sat down.

"What is it?" Romeo asked.

"I. . . I'm getting a scholarship anyway, it would seem." Camille rested the letter on her lap and looked up at Romeo, hating the tears behind her eyes.

Romeo scrambled into the chair next to Camille and pulled her hands into his. "I won't stand in your way. This is your dream."

A tear slid down her cheek, and she smiled. "No, it's not. It was Alexa's dream for me to be like her. I'm tired of chasing that."

"Then why are you crying?"

Camille sniffled and laughed. "Because I finally know what I want. I found the truth under the redwood tree. It's been in front of me all this time."

Romeo's brows wrinkled. "And?"

Aware that everyone was waiting for some sort of profound answer from her, Camille exhaled and continued. "Some have said the song 'Under the Greenwood Tree' is about the wonders and beauty of nature, taking the time to enjoy life, to not get caught up in ambition and riches that can never satisfy."

"So. . . ?" Romeo asked.

"I love it here. How could I ever leave?" Camille leaned closer, her lips almost touching his. "And I love you, Romeo. How could I ever leave you?"

"Cara mia, ti voglio bene." Romeo slid his hands through her hair, cupping her cheeks. "My darling, I love you."

Then he kissed her.

A Letter To Our Readers

Dear Reader:

In order that we might better contribute to your reading enjoyment, we would appreciate your taking a few minutes to respond to the following questions. We welcome your comments and read each form and letter we receive. When completed, please return to the following:

Fiction Editor
Heartsong Presents
PO Box 719
Uhrichsville, Ohio 44683

1. Did you enjoy reading *Under the Redwood Tree* by Elizabeth Goddard?
   ❏ Very much! I would like to see more books by this author!
   ❏ Moderately. I would have enjoyed it more if

   _____

   _____

   _____

2. Are you a member of **Heartsong Presents**? ❏ Yes ❏ No
   If no, where did you purchase this book? _____

   _____

3. How would you rate, on a scale from 1 (poor) to 5 (superior), the cover design? _____

4. On a scale from 1 (poor) to 10 (superior), please rate the following elements.

   ____ Heroine   ____ Plot
   ____ Hero   ____ Inspirational theme
   ____ Setting   ____ Secondary characters

5. These characters were special because? _____

_____

_____

6. How has this book inspired your life? _____

_____

_____

7. What settings would you like to see covered in future
   Heartsong Presents books? _____

_____

_____

8. What are some inspirational themes you would like to see
   treated in future books? _____

_____

_____

9. Would you be interested in reading other **Heartsong
   Presents** titles? ❏ Yes ❏ No

10. Please check your age range:
    ❏ Under 18   ❏ 18-24
    ❏ 25-34   ❏ 35-45
    ❏ 46-55   ❏ Over 55

Name _____

Occupation _____

Address _____

City, State, Zip _____

E-mail _____